Brothers of Vengeance

Brothers of Vengeance

LAURAN PAINE

Sagebrush

Large Print Westerns

Library of Congress Cataloging-in-Publication Data

Paine, Lauran.
    Brothers of vengeance / Lauran Paine.
        p.   cm.
        ISBN 1-57490-495-7 (alk. paper)
    1. Arizona—Fiction. 2. Large type books. I. Title.

PS3566.A34B76 2003
813'.54—dc21   2003010604

Cataloging in Publication Data is available from
the British Library and the National Library of Australia.

Sagebrush Large Print Westerns are published in the United
States and Canada by Thomas T. Beeler, Publisher, PO Box 659,
Hampton Falls, New Hampshire 03844-0659. ISBN 1-57490-495-7

Published in the United Kingdom, Eire, and the Republic of
South Africa by Isis Publishing Ltd, 7 Centremead, Osney
Mead, Oxford OX2 0ES England. ISBN 0-7531-6918-5

Published in Australia and New Zealand by Bolinda Publishing
Pty Ltd, 17 Mohr Street, Tullamarine, Victoria, Australia, 3043
ISBN 1-74030-925-1

Manufactured by Sheridan Books in Chelsea, Michigan.

Brothers of Vengeance

CHAPTER ONE

IT WAS THE FIRST GOOD WARMTH AFTER WINTER with the redbuds swollen with fresh sap and larks saucily singing in the meadow. A band of lice-infested Indians had passed four days earlier, their bony nags shuffling along, each rider wrapped in a filthy old blanket, some with pups on their backs or riding painfully astride skinny withers, held there by black-eyed squaws while the bucks sat straight and apart, rifles cased in beaded buckhide scabbards. Once, such a migration towards the high country where Indians summered, struck fear and awe, now all it struck was contempt and perhaps, with some, a little pity. They were the dispossessed. No one understood them; they were unlike everyone else. Still; they were people; they could suffer and grieve just like other folks, even if they were filthy redskins.

Evelyn Hunter came down the roadway without lifting a bit of dust, riding that spotted mare she set such store by which had once belonged to redskins; its ears had been split straight up on each side, then the separate halves rolled and tied until they'd healed into two little stiff balls of curled hair, a pair of those little odd-looking balls on each side. It was an odd sight, but then, redskins had odd notions of what enhanced beauty.

Evelyn was a tall girl with dark, straight brows that came close to meeting above her gunmetal eyes and her straight, high-bridged nose. She was long-legged and high-breasted with a wide, full mouth, and although her skin was fair, especially after the bleak winter, and her hair was ash blonde, she had a dark look to her; it was her eyes, large and solemn and unsmiling, which lent

1

her that darkness. And it may also have been her way, because Evelyn had her gloomy side.

She'd once been married to a man named Axel Hunter, but he'd been killed in a skirmish with bronco bucks some years back. She was twenty-five years of age or thereabouts and lived with her elderly father on the Hunter place upcountry three miles from the Colburn homestead.

Marci Colburn was eighteen, but she was the only other female in a long day's ride that was anywhere near Evelyn Hunter's age. Still; they made a strange pair. Marci was sturdy and not so tall. She laughed easily and had a way of laying her head slightly to one side, then looking up mischievously, that had half the rangeriders in the Tanawha Valley ready to leap into double harness. But Marci was also shrewd and independent— and headstrong.

She was full-breasted and sturdy through the middle with legs as nut-brown and muscular as the legs of a young boy. She wore her red-auburn hair close cropped, also like a boy, and sat a horse like she'd been born to one, which wasn't common among settlers. And she looked straight at things; there was a directness to her that was a mite unsettling, even to Evelyn, who knew the way of men and their hungry thoughts.

Still, when Evelyn reined over into the yard, Marci came from the house brightening with recognition and warm friendliness, because, ill-assorted though they were, they had some things in common. Mainly, it had been a hard winter and Marci had paced the cabin like a trapped thing hungering for springtime and her freedom. She had that kind of mercurial disposition that frets under restraint and wilts from inactivity.

She ran from the rear stoop out into the golden-

2

lighted yard and laughed up at the older woman, who was dismounting. "Sure sign of spring," she called. "You coming down the road, Evelyn. How's your paw?"

Evelyn led the horse to a spindly tree and tied it there. "He came through," she said, solemn. "The cold season was long this year, Marci. How's your maw an' brother?"

"Fine. They're fine. Come on inside, maw'll be happy to see you. Sam's out hunting, but you didn't want to see him anyway."

"No," murmured Evelyn, looking across at the chinked log house with its solid squareness and its little spindrift of watery smoke rising from the mud-wattle chimney. She hesitated, dropping her gaze to Marci. "You wintered good," she stated.

"I'm glad it's past," said Marci. "I love the springs and summers, even the autumns sometimes, but not the winters. Come along; maw'll be glad to see you."

They walked over and entered the house, which was a hewn-log structure created some time long past by wise and powerful hands knowledgeable in the ways of squaring logs and notching corners. It was a house built to endure, almost as though its careful builder had kept some deep secret within himself about this house: That it must serve his family after he was gone, and so it was serving them, for John Colburn had died two seasons past of the lung fever in this same sturdy house. He lay now over beyond the log barn he'd also created, in a hallowed place behind a rude picket fence, put up hastily by his survivors to keep the cattle from trampling through, beside a small mound where his baby son also lay.

There were some log corrals around the barn, from

back to the off-side, which was southerly, also carefully constructed, for the cattle in northern Arizona Territory went wild after a year or two of free-running the endless unfenced range. Nothing short of powerful stringers and massive posts would hold them in.

The land ran on westerly, behind the house and barn, gently rising and falling, interspersed with trees here and there, and occasionally, upon the lip of some shallow, broad erosion arroyo, speckled with spiny brush that was endemic and which seemed to flourish despite long winters and wilting summers.

Water was the main thing. Some of the cowmen who'd been in the Tanawha Valley since Indian times had springs or dug-wells that flowed year round, but the latecomers, the emigrant settlers, were rarely that fortunate. Old Man Hunter, for example, had a dug well that gave out brown soup every late summer; it was hoarded for the cattle. For domestic use Hunter and his daughter loaded barrels in a wagon and drove seven miles to a seepage spring someone had long ago dug out and rocked-up, there to fill their barrels by bucket and return homeward. Late summer was, for many, a miserable time.

Northward, where the mountains stood cool and gloomy, folks hunted for the winter meat they salted or jerked, and stored away. But never alone because the Indians roamed up there, and vanquished or not, lone hunters had a way of riding up in there and never returning.

There was a town, Minton, four miles eastward. It was a cowtown; rough and crude and thriving. It tolerated emigrants because they only appeared there to spend money for flour or sugar or salt and soda, but it was the cattlemen's town, so settlers were not very

4

welcome in it.

Sometimes, a wagonload of emigrant men would drive in after round-up or before haying time, and not be molested. But the feeling was there in Minton, that this was a horseman's world; sod-busters weren't welcome.

Still, the bad days were past when men died in their fields or had cattle run across their crops. When emigrants waylaid rangeriders and shot them out of their saddles. The Army had come two years earlier and ended all that with five hangings and heavy-handed patrolling. Gun-heavy cowboys were scarce now, and sod-busters went to their fields leaving rifles behind. Progress, some said, was coming, and with it came book-law to replace gun-law.

What really ended the sputtering range war was prosperity; the cattle market had been good for three years. The rich cattlemen got richer and the settlers went to bed each night with full bellies. It was the prosperity which made the truce permanent. Still; the disapproval, the suspicions, the hard looks, were still there if a man wanted to look for them.

As long as good times lasted, no one particularly looked for trouble; no one had the time. Winter run-off brought up plentiful grass. Cattle got greasy fat and calved-out with a high percentage of survival. This kept settlers and cowmen alike busy through marking time, through haying time for the sod-busters—the big cattlemen put up no hay—and it also kept the men in the saddle trying to control the natural drift of animals which had no reason to stay close when there was water and feed anywhere they chose to ramble.

There was even a kind of easy comradeship when the rangemen and sod-busters met far out, hunting strays or gathering herds at the marking grounds to be branded

5

and altered and earmarked. Some of the sod-busters became tophands; some were good cattlemen, and honest. It was difficult, in prosperous times, to dislike an honest man.

As Mike Hunter, Evelyn's father, once told old Hubert Hathaway, owner of the HH outfit, "Give most men a chance, Mister Hathaway, and you'll find they're not much different from you. There are only two kinds of people in this world—the good an' the bad. An' it's always the good ones that do the judging."

What had initially sparked bad blood had been elemental hunger. The big cow outfits had thousands of head of beef. The emigrants arrived in Tanawha Valley with old wagons, bony teams, big-eyed womenfolk and scrawny children. The most honest man alive will not remain honest if, to keep the dull apathy of hunger from his family's eyes, he has only to step to the door and shoot a rich man's cow to fill his larder.

Hathaway once told Sheriff Markley over at Minton that he didn't mind the loss of a cow or two to keep someone's kids from starving; what he got angry about was when he rode the range and saw an HH cow suckling a calf with some settlers' brand on it, fresh and pink. "That," stated Bert Hathaway, "is just plain rustling, Tom Markley, and if you don't handle it, I will!"

No one denied that was how most of the sod-busters got their start in the cow business, not even the settlers themselves. But no one made light of it either, for cow stealing, like horse stealing, was a capital crime punishable by death. That was what had started the night riding a few years back; some rangerider found a mismatched pair, told his employer, and some moonless night there was a knock on a settler's door. When the man opened it, with glowing lamplight behind him, he was shot down from out in the darkness, and of course the shod-horse tracks were found each following morning, to serve as fair warning to other sod-busters.

But the Army ended all that. The feeling was still there, especially in places like Minton where the rangemen sometimes took on a bigger load of Valley Tan than was good for them at the saloons, but generally, with the advent of good times there was very little squabbling any more.

It was a big land. From the northward hills southward to the Rosebud Basin, five hundred miles of open range supported some thirty thousand cattle with room left over for three times that many more, when one looked east and west where more free-graze ran, farther than a man could ride in a month. Tanawha Valley was larger than many European countries; with the Indians thinned down to a few skulking, scavenging bands, with prosperity abroad, with low mutterings but no longer any actual organized ill will, it promised to be a good springtime, the third year after the passing of Marci's father, sturdy John Colburn.

His wife had no reason to believe otherwise, that golden day Evelyn Hunter rode down to call. She was a grey woman lined with her share of hardship but with an enduring twinkle that no amount of agony could entirely dim. She was a handsome woman, in her forties, with some vague but noticeable affinity with her handsome daughter; she too was solid-built and strong, with the brown coloring of health and the clear vision of an unconquerable spirit.

Her name was Mary, as her mother's name had been before her, and also her grandmother's name. She was originally from the Carolinas, but had gone early to

Missouri when she'd married John Colburn. From there, the way to Arizona Territory had been long and marked with travail. Now, at last settled, she had buried a baby son and her husband. She would never leave Tanawha Valley; her two strongest loves lay buried here. Her surviving children, Marci and young Sam, belonged here. She was content.

CHAPTER TWO

ORDINARILY, SOD-BUSTERS CAME IN A CLUTCH; of all the settlers who'd arrived in the Tanawha country in the past six or seven years, only the Gunn brothers came without wives or pups. At first, when the bad blood had marred the days and nights, folks made fun of that name, but before the Army finally squelched the shooting, there were no longer any settlers, or cattlemen either, who laughed.

Langston Gunn was a grave, strong man who did not often laugh. He was an even six feet in height and had solid gristle packed under a smooth, tough hide. He was brown-eyed and brown-haired, which contrasted with the coloring of his brother, Henry, who seemed to be seven or eight years younger and was fair. They were different in other ways too. Henry was a born horseman. He could out-ride most of the rangemen and when it came to winnowing the meanness out of a horse, Henry had the hands and the temperament for it.

Langston was an inward man. Henry could smile and laugh. Langston worked silently, Henry often sang or whistled. But they shared another attribute—both were deadly with guns; both were seasoned in all the things it took to be good stockmen.

8

Even the cattlemen never said the Gunn brothers stole cattle, not even at the height of the feuding. But still, although they settled well away from the other sod-busters, they were emigrants, and this had placed them squarely upon the side of the emigrants when trouble had come.

Except for the Gunn brothers, Hubert Hathaway had once darkly exclaimed, the emigrants would have hitched up and pulled out, after the first one was killed by nightriders.

Tom Markley was certain in his heart it had been the Gunn brothers who had evened up the score with weapons for the settlers, but he'd never been able to prove it. But Markley kept a wary eye on Langston; he'd known that quiet, uncompromising type before. They could be killed but they could not be vanquished any other way.

After the trouble—two years afterwards in fact because it took that long for the cattlemen to unbend against those two—young Henry was hired by the big outfits to take the snap out of green colts. He wouldn't do it at the cow camps though; they had to fetch the horses to the Gunn place. One year later the rangemen were willing in all fairness to admit, there wasn't a bronc-stomper in the whole Tanawha country who could hold a candle to him. When he turned them back they weren't just broke, they were also reined.

About Langston, though, there was no unanimity of opinion. Those who'd seen him angry swore he was a professional gunfighter. Those who'd had reason to back off in the face of his dark stare, said that whether he was a professional or not, he didn't know the meaning of the word fear.

But Langston Gunn's reputation was a blessing, too;

9

unless the cattlemen had reason to ride over and talk, they left him entirely alone. He inspired that kind of respect with his unsmiling, dead-level gaze and his seeming total lack of humor, or need for companionable small talk.

"A loner," Bert Hathaway told Tom Markley in Minton, one time. "That one's a loner. He's the kind that'd ride up to your front door, call you out and put a bullet through your skull without battin' an eye."

Tom had privately agreed, but he'd kept his opinion to himself, for after the trouble was past, Langston Gunn seldom ever came to Minton. Henry did, quite often when he was putting miles under some green colt, but Langston rode in only when he had good reason, and he never lingered after he'd accomplished what he'd come for.

All anyone knew about the Gunn brothers was that they were Texans. Rumor had it that Langston had been a high officer in the Secesh army during the Civil War, but that was only a rumor. In a country like northern Arizona Territory where the winters were bitterly long, rumors flourished.

When the settlers had trouble at calving time or with marking and altering, they sent for the Gunn brothers. It was no secret they were experienced stockmen. The only *real* stockmen among the emigrants; all the others had been farmers.

There was a world of difference.

The spring John Colburn left his family there was a rash of trouble at the calving grounds. Some said there was water hemlock near the waterholes to cause it, others said it was simply because it had been too wet a spring. No one actually knew what caused it. All folks knew was that first-calf heifers were dying like flies at

10

calving, and even fourth- and fifth-calf cows had trouble. An old Kentuckian who rode through the country said it was because the moon was in a wrong quarter for calving-out. A few were reserved in their judgment about that; none cared to agree openly it might be so yet not everyone scoffed, either.

It was into its second week before they sent for Langston and Henry Gunn. They were all calved out, they said, upon arriving, and if the others would lend a hand at watching so, their critters didn't drift too far, they'd be glad to make the rounds.

They worked as a team, rarely speaking. They'd ride the range until they found a critter down, then go to work. If the calf was coming backward, Langston who had the greatest talent for it, would roll up both sleeves to his shoulders, go in, turn the calf, get its forelegs started right, set his booted feet against the critter's flank-bones and heave. If he couldn't do it they'd use lariats and a saddle horse. Sometimes the calves were starting right, forelegs first, head down and pushed forward, but there just wasn't enough leeway. In these cases it was almost invariably a first-calf heifer. They'd get the calf out then go sit in the shade and have a smoke, waiting, because sometimes heifers struggled to their feet and staggered off, abandoning their calves.

Langston knew the way of it, though. They would deliver as many as forty calves a day, and scarcely lose one. It went like that for twenty-seven days, or until they'd pulled so many calves Henry said he was forgetting what human beings looked like.

On the twenty-eighth day they found two HH heifers down with forelegs and heads out, not eighty rods apart. They pulled the calves and settled the cows, then waited, washing at a little creek nearby through the

11

trees. When they sauntered back both heifers were up, licking their babies. Different men get their rewards in this life different ways. Langston's dark eyes glowed and Henry smiled. Neither of them saw the horsemen until they walked on out of the trees.

There were four of them, three rangehands and one snow-thatched, brown-faced wizened beanstalk of an older man sitting atop a handsome chestnut horse with a rusty mane and tail. Bert Hathaway.

The cowman pointed at the solicitous heifers trying to nuzzle their calves away from the men on horses with low sounds and anxious looks. "You fellers pull those calves?" he asked.

Langston was rolling down his sleeves when he said, "Yes. Any objections, Mister Hathaway?"

The cowman considered Langston longest. "No objection at all, Mister Gunn. As a matter of fact I'm obliged to you."

"For what, Mister Hathaway; weren't any HH riders around. We were. The heifers were hung up and flat down." Langston finished with his sleeves and looked up at the older man. "You'd do as much for settler heifers, wouldn't you, if there wasn't any help around?"

Hathaway was slow answering that. He seemed to be wondering whether or not Langston Gunn was being sarcastic. "I'm a good neighbor," he eventually exclaimed, skirting a direct answer. "If folks are the same to me, Mister Gunn."

Henry, standing easy before those four, regarded the cowboys rather than their employer. "Charley," he said to one of them, "is there any drift beyond the plum thickets?"

A leathery, beard-stubbled rough man riding a jet-black ridgling, flung his head from side to side. "We ain't seen any, Henry. We rode out thataway week ago."

Bert Hathaway dropped a grave look upon the younger Gunn, lifting his rein-hand and saying nothing. Langston stepped over to his horse, thumbed under the cincha then rose up over leather. Henry followed that example. The pair of them exchanged a solemn nod with the HH men and rode off at a slow walk without gazing back.

There was no bad blood, actually, but hard men come to manhood in a hard land sometimes had long memories. Only three years earlier if they'd met like that, the chances would have been better than even someone would have started shooting.

"Damned old coot," Henry said, when they skirted a low hill where trees grew in a gloomy fringe atop it, "he acts like he expects trouble all the time."

"That's just his way," retorted Langston, looking around for more down cows. "He's been at it a long time; men his age don't just shake hands and start over clean. They aren't made that way."

"Any more'n you are," muttered Henry, and shrugged when Langston looked around.

They weren't far south of the foothills and the day was well spent. Their own holdings lay on easterly five or six miles. If they'd wished they could've pushed on and slept in their bunks, but they didn't. They had bedrolls and jerky. They knew where a white-water creek was up in this northward country. Besides, with spring upon the land the nights were benign. Not warm, exactly, but not bitter cold either.

They reached the white-water and off-saddled a hundred or so yards from where the first dark stands of big timber rolled upwards and away upon the yonder slopes. Their camp was established in a bend of the

13

creek where some white oaks stood back a little distance, casting thick shadows, and where some cottonwoods grew closer to the creek bank. It was a pleasant spot. It was also secluded enough to pass unnoticed unless it were really sought after.

They made an early fire for coffee, sat relaxed while they ate, and afterwards spread their blankets. It was a good time for solitary men after a rewarding day. They lounged there talking a little now and then, and silent for long periods too.

"Pulled close to fifty today," Henry said, just before the last red blaze of sunlight flashed out from beyond the peaks. "If it happens next spring maybe we ought to take young Sam Colburn and one or two others, show them how it's done, and have several teams out working at the same time."

Langston was agreeable. "Good notion," he agreed. "Time young Sam got some education."

"Sure admire that sister of his," murmured Henry, easing down with a quiet groan upon his blankets. "She sure sets a man's heart to pounding."

Langston's wide mouth lifted faintly at the outer corners. "Springtime," he murmured. "The sap's running. Well; tomorrow we might as well go on back across our own range. Calved out but still, we've been out near a month."

"Hey, Lang; recollect that long-legged Eller girl back at Pecos?"

Langston unbuckled his gun-belt, carefully wrapped it and lay the holstered pistol close to his right side as he also lay back upon his soogans. The dusky evening was fast falling. "Got no reason to forget her," he said. "You goin' to talk all night, or go to sleep?"

"Wonder whatever became of those Ellers, Lang?"

14

"Who knows? The war uprooted lots of folks. Look where we landed—Arizona Territory."

"We could've done a heap worse!"

"Maybe. But where a man grows up is where by all rights he ought to stay. It's like the Comanches used to say; they'd die fighting for their hunting grounds, but more than that, a man shouldn't abandon the graves and bones of his people."

Henry watched the stars firm up one at a time through cottonwood limbs. "There wasn't much left to stay home for, Lang. When the Yanks pulled out what was left of Pecos?"

Langston sighed and pushed out his legs to their full length, set his battered hat aside and looked over into the dusky east where a jagged skyline showed pale against the sooty heavens.

"Amnesty," he murmured. "Amnesty and a rock-ranch. It wasn't much, was it? Still; a man's got roots, sort of like a tree; they don't pull up easy, Henry. For you maybe but not for me."

Henry raised up on one elbow. "You want to go back?" he asked quickly.

"No. Folks can't go back. If they try it never works. It's just a haunt. That's all. But I'm older; I remember more things. Sometimes it's like yesterday, Henry. Other times it's like a bad dream that's sort of hazy and bitter. Sometimes I can close my eyes hard and see the folks' graves behind the paling fence. And the house, the way it used to be, not the way it looked after those Yank soldiers fired it." Langston heaved restlessly upon his blankets. "What the hell are we talkin' like this for?" He growled, his voice roughening. "Go to sleep. We pulled a heap of calves today. The settlers'll be happy when they see 'em."

Henry watched his brother roll upon his far side, his face towards the dark slopes and distant peaks, and gently eased back down.

Langston was a lot like their father had been. Solemn most of the time, quiet, with a powerful urge to spend his days in the service of the soil, in the service of living dumb things. A grave, rawboned, powerful man soured on mankind and seasoned in the ways of violence. He recalled how Langston had ridden off to war, unsmiling, and how he'd returned, still unsmiling, but leaner and quieter, three years later, scarred and gaunt and burnt black from many fiery suns, astride a big bay horse with a U.S. brand on its neck and a Yankee saddle under his Secesh britches.

A world had ended during those three years; Henry had come of age, but too late. It was all over by the time he was ready to also take his stand.

He yawned and blinked at the overhead sky. Well; Arizona was his land now, and whatever Fate had in store for him, was still ahead.

CHAPTER THREE

THEY SAW A FLYING WEDGE OF GEESE PASS ACROSS in a clean sweep the following day; their honking came down to the warming range with a melancholy echo. The sky was leaden, hiding the sun, pretending winter hadn't passed quite yet, rolls of dirty grey hurrying along under pressure from a high, silent wind. But it was warm for all the storm signals when they broke camp, rigged out and started riding.

"The last cold rain," mused Henry, watching those low banks of soiled grey pass directly overhead. "Now

16

the grass will grow."

They left the creek heading southeastward. Far ahead through the gunmetal day they saw dust hanging in the stillness where a stage had raced southward towards Minton. Otherwise, except for occasional bunches of fattening cattle, the land was empty.

They passed a mound of stones Langston had erected when they'd first squatted on their home-place. It was a boundary marker. Everything west was HH, everything east as far as the stage road and for a mile beyond, was Gunn range. They also passed a scooped out place where the earth was bleached from many fires. In years past Indians had traditionally camped in this place. No one, Indians or others, had camped here now for a long time.

They spotted some critters bearing a large letter G seared into their ribs on the right side, and wordlessly counted calves. No one ever calved out one hundred per cent; seventy per cent was usual. With all things favorable, a man might now and then achieve eighty or ninety percent, but not often. Particularly with an occasional old gummer wolf sneaking down out of the northward mountains where he was too old and slow to catch deer, percentages were held down.

Henry saw wolf sign and pointed it out. Langston looked and nodded. Before haying time they'd have a hunt. The settlers banded together for that kind of a sweep every year. It was the only way to keep down the predator population.

They saw their log house while still more than a mile out. They passed eight of their horses, too, and even the older ones threw up their heads, snorted, lifted their tails and raced away as though they'd never before in all their lives seen men. The only time old horses acted like

17

that was when they were feeling good.

Two riders loped up from the south, bearing off on a westerly tangent with the grey day making every detail clear. Henry looked a long time. Langston looked too, but after he'd satisfied himself he found other, closer, more pertinent things to consider. Not Henry. He kept watching even after he had to twist around in the saddle, so finally Langston dryly said, "Females. Girls. Well; one's not so much of a girl any more, but she's still female."

Henry straightened around and wordlessly rode on. They were close to the barn which was not quite completed yet, before Henry said, "Pretty far from home, if it should come a cloudburst."

Langston rode on up, stepped down, lifted his nose and sniffed, and shook his head. "No rain today. Maybe tonight or tomorrow if that high wind doesn't blow the clouds off, but not today." He bent to the unsaddling, his face grave and composed, and thoughtful. "Anyway; those two've been riding this range long enough. They'll have slickers."

Henry dropped his saddle, led his horse across to a corral and turned him in. He held the gate, waiting. When Langston came over he said, "Kind of hard on those Colburns, John dying like that leaving them alone."

Langston turned his horse in, seized the gate and closed it. He draped his bridle over a post and spat. He needed a shave and a bath. "They've made fair enough so far," he exclaimed indifferently, eyeing the unfinished side of their barn. "Three, four more good years and young Sam'll be big enough to take over where John left off. Maybe, after we clean up, we could put in a little time on the barn."

They walked to the house. It was three large rooms; a

18

kitchen big enough to cook and eat in, a large parlor with a huge mud-wattle fireplace, and a bedroom, also very large. There was nothing attractive about the place. At most of the claims womenfolk had dressed up the windows with sack curtains; had planted geraniums or set out willow-slips. The Gunn ranch had no women and therefore it was ugly. The buildings were good enough; not as well-built as John Colburn's buildings, but then neither Langston nor Henry knew much about construction, except perhaps corral and barn construction. But everything was solid and tight and strongly dowelled. The Gunn buildings would stand a long time; they were functional, big, and raw looking without any frills such as the stoop and porch most settler-men had made in front of their entrances.

But there was water. That was why the Gunn place was so far from the other squatter-ranches. Langston and Henry were experienced stockmen. They'd looked first for water, then for good range with strong grass and low hills for critters to bed down behind when the winds and the snows came.

It had required a lot of dynamite to blast out their spring upon the westerly sidehill, and it had also taken considerable sweat to ditch it down by gravity-flow to their barnyard troughs and on over to the house. Without the money for piping they'd spent two winters burning cores out of saplings to form enough hollowed-out logs to bring water into the house. They had the only ranch for some distance with a bung-starter jutting from a log wall which, when opened, let water rush into their corrugated kitchen sink.

"Stoke the fire," Langston said, flinging aside his hat. "I'll get the razors. Look like a cub bear an' I can't look any better."

19

They shaved and cleaned up. When that was done it was early afternoon, the scudding clouds were breaking up, and off in the west a golden shaft of dazzling sunlight shone where a little rainbow lay, far out over HH range.

They went back out to spend the remainder of the day at their constant chore—finishing the log barn. There was a sturdy scaffolding along the north side. Henry climbed up wordlessly and Langston began raising peeled, split timbers to lay upright upon the scaffolding's edge so that Henry could haul them up to bore holes and lift into place for dowelling. It was a monotonous chore, never different. For a barn as large as the one they were building, a lot of man-hours were required, and mostly, they worked in silence. There wasn't much to discuss beyond the weather, the condition of the stock, the prospects for another good year, all subjects they'd long since exhausted. There was small talk, gossip, speculation, but Langston was the wrong man for that. He only spoke when he had something to say.

While Henry worked high up, Langston finished stacking the available timbers and went over to split more. They had a month earlier with snow still lying in protected places, barked their logs. Barking went faster when there was frost in the air.

They'd made dowels through the winter in their kitchen with the wind blowing and the snow piling up, sipping coffee beside the popping cook-stove. They had more than enough dowels.

Henry's thick shoulders hunched each time he had to muscle a log into place. When they were particularly heavy he'd grunt and perhaps swear. But it was a good kind of labor, and each time he took a breather leaning upon the fresh siding, he could see all around.

They had a hayfield, as did all the settlers. It was fenced to keep out livestock and bristly with pale stalks of the previous summer's cutting. The land was richly deep and dark-moldy in color. Men like Hubert Hathaway put up no hay; they didn't have to. Only when stockmen were limited by the size of their holdings did they have to save out part of the land to raise winter feed upon. HH simply reserved their best protected range for winter feed, drifted the cattle on to this range after the first freeze, and while no animal got fat on stem-cured grass, it kept them alive and strong enough to get through the winters. Unless they were old gummer cows, in which case they sometimes died if the snowdrifts got too deep.

Henry bent, caught hold of another split log and hoisted it upwards hand over hand until he could turn and lay it full length of the scaffolding before raising it into place. More and more of those scudding dirty clouds broke up, allowing the sun to shine through. There was a hazy, reddish tint to the late day brightness. In wintertime it was dark by four o'clock. In springtime the darkness came like smoke, making a haze which lasted until five or six before it was time to head for the house and light a lamp. Two months from now with full summer upon the land, darkness wouldn't settle until around nine o'clock. That was when they'd finish the barn because the days would start earlier and end later.

Henry bent, grasped his log, straightened slowly and pressed the thing up even with his chin, rocked it into place atop the lower length of siding, and paused to expel a burst of pent-up breath. From below Langston said, "We're going to have to raise the scaffolding directly, Henry."

It took a moment to set and drive the first dowel pin, to work carefully along holding the log into place as far as the next hole where another dowel was set. After that, the log couldn't fall and knock Henry off his perch, so he took his time. He got to the far right-hand end and set the dowel, raised the sledge, and turned his head for no reason to sweep the westerly range with a look before driving in the wooden pin. He held the hammer poised without bringing it down. Langston, watching from below, looked up, then swung to also gaze westward. But Langston was on the ground, his view cut off by the low hills, so he called up.

"What do you see, Henry?"

Very slowly Henry lowered the sledge, struck the dowel, looked off westerly again and finally dropped the hammer. "Rider. Maybe a mile out on the far side of the low hill where the spring is."

Langston looked again and shrugged. It wasn't at all unusual for rangemen to be riding out, even this late in the day. "Finish setting that pin," he exclaimed, and stooped to set his splitting wedges.

"He's not riding his horse, though. He's leading it. He's staggerin' around like he's drunk, Lang."

Langston straightened up, wiped both hands down the side of his trousers and lifted his head. "Recognize him?" he asked.

"No. He's pokin' along leadin' his horse. Hey; I'll bet he's hurt." Henry turned and started hand over hand down off the scaffolding. When he hit the ground he said, "Come on; let's ride out there. Might be snake-bit or bucked off, or something. He's sure wanderin' around like something's wrong."

They saddled up fast, got astride, and left the yard in a long lope, bearing northward up and around that first

22

low hill. Langston finally spotted the horseman. He was a good mile off and stumbling along southward, his horse following on a loose rein.

He signaled for his brother to slacken his pace. Henry obeyed but he kept sitting straight up, straining forward, his expression anxious and troubled. Langston, reverting to the caution which had developed in him down the years when approaching a strange rider, even one in obvious trouble, let his mount walk along while he intently observed that rider far ahead.

The horse being led along wasn't limping; neither did he act snorty as a bucking horse would have. The man out front seemed sound in the limbs too. At least he neither limped nor held his swinging arms stiff. What interested Langston when they got closer was that he could make out no belt-gun around the stranger's middle and no Winchester booted to the saddle. It wasn't unusual for unarmed riders to be abroad, but it wasn't common either.

"He's unarmed," Langston said, booting out his mount. "Let's go."

They raced ahead, riding close together, and finally got close enough to make out that their stranger wasn't a man at all, it was a girl, and she wasn't a stranger. It was Evelyn Hunter. Henry ripped out her name and spurred away from Langston. He got up close, left his saddle in a flying leap and ran the last fifty feet. Langston came up slower. As he dismounted he saw Evelyn Hunter collapse against his brother. From habit Langston hung back, turned completely around studying the empty land all around, and didn't go on over to the girl and Henry until he was satisfied there were no other riders anywhere close by.

Henry twisted, his face anxious. "She fainted," he

23

said. "She must be bad hurt, Lang. We better get her to the house."

Langston shook his head and pointed. "Lay her flat," he ordered. "If she's bad hurt hauling her around won't make her any better. Lay her flat down."

Henry obeyed. The brothers knelt, gazing at the girl. There was no sign of blood or injury. Henry suddenly flung up his head. "Marci," he rapped out. "When we saw her riding earlier, Marci Colburn was with her. That must be it, Lang. Something's happened to Marci."

Langston's brows dropped straight down in a solemn look of perplexity. He put forth a hand to brush back a lock of tumbled ash blonde hair. The girl's eyelids faintly moved. "She's coming around, Henry. I don't see any sign of hurt."

"Well it was sure somethin'."

Langston slowly nodded, bent low and said, "Miss Evelyn; can you hear me now? Miss Evelyn; what happened?"

The girl's eyes flew wide open at the sound of that deep, low voice close to her face. She flung up an arm as though to ward off something. Langston caught her hand and held it.

"What is it?" he asked. "What's wrong?"

She formed a silent word, her eyes growing large and glassily staring. "Dead. He was dead. Hanging there—dead!"

CHAPTER FOUR

THEY GOT HER TO THE HOUSE before she made any sense at all, and for the last quarter mile of that ride with darkness settling in, she clasped the saddlehorn with

24

both hands staring ahead, ash-grey around the mouth.

Langston tossed aside his hat and helped Henry get her through into their big kitchen, after that, while Henry spoke low and soothingly, Langston put the coffee pot on to boil, stoked up the fire and lit a lamp which he put upon the oilcloth-covered table. Evelyn was nearly as rigid now as she'd been loose and near collapse before.

Langston stood back considering the girl. Something had shaken her down to the roots. Someone was dead, he'd figured that much out, but the part about someone hanging there meant simply that someone dead had been found hanging up in a bush, possibly, where she had seen him. Langston went to the stove, turned his back and while neither the girl nor Henry could see, he poured a liberal lacing of rye whisky into one of the cups. Afterwards, he filled three cups and returned to the table. She was sobbing now. Leaning against Henry's shoulder sobbing.

Langston was careful about how he placed the cups. Henry noticed that as he eased the girl back and reached for his bandanna to wipe her cheeks. He handed her the black coffee.

"Drink up, Miss Evelyn," Henry said. "Drink up then tell us exactly what's wrong."

Langston eased down across the table and impassively studied the girl. When he saw color come, saw her eyes gradually warm to a steady brightness, he gently inclined his head at her.

"Now, from the beginning," he said. "Henry and I saw you and Marci Colburn riding northwesterly this afternoon when we were riding for home. After that, what happened?"

Evelyn looked over at somber Langston, where

butter-yellow lamp glow fell across his lean, sun-blackened features with their rock-steady dark eyes. She drew in a big breath and shatteringly let it out. "Marci's still out there with him," she said in a fading tone.

"All right," retorted Langston, pointing. "Drink the rest of the coffee." He watched her obediently reach out. "Marci's still out there with who, ma'am?"

She drained the cup. "With her brother; with Sam."

Henry leaned back in his chair to stare. Langston too, widened his steady gaze. "You mean—it was young Sam Colburn you girls found hangin' in a bush on the range, dead?"

"No bush," Evelyn said, with a vigorous headshake. "He was hanging from a tree—by a rope."

Henry stiffened. "Lynched . . .? Are you sayin' someone hanged young Sam Colburn, Miss Evelyn?"

She put aside the cup, nodding. The brothers saw her painfully swallow. "Yes. It was a lariat. He was hanging there turning from side to side very slowly. His rifle was broken over a rock close by and there was no sign of his horse."

For a full minute there wasn't a sound. Langston brought his big, scarred hands together atop the table and clasped them. Henry loosened a little in his chair, gazing straight at the girl.

"Are you sure?" inquired Langston quietly. "Miss Evelyn; are you plumb certain it was young Sam Colburn, and that he was hanging by his neck from a tree?"

"Yes. Oh, Mister Gunn, *yes*!" A shudder passed the full length of her as she rapidly blinked at Langston.

Henry said softly, "Now get hold of yourself, Miss Evelyn. Get hold of yourself. You can cry later. Right now tell me—where is he—and where is Miss Marci?"

26

"She—I already told you; she stayed up there with him. I started for home—for somewhere—for anywhere—to get help. Then I got sick to my stomach and afterwards I started walking. I—"

"Ma'am," broke in Langston, "can you take us up there where he's hangin' and where you left Miss Marci?"

Evelyn swallowed again and nodded. Langston looked at his clasped hands. He was privately considering contingencies.

"It's dark out now," he murmured. "Can you find the spot in the dark?"

"Yes. Marci and I go riding often, when the weather is good. We sometimes go to that place because it's close to the white-water creek. I can find it."

"All right," stated Langston, uncoiling up off the chair. "Now one more question: Was there anyone else up there when you found Sam?"

"No. There was no one up there. It was so quiet . . ."

"Sure," Langston swiftly said, and jerked his head at Henry. "You help her out to the barn while I get us a couple of Winchesters."

Outside, the last of the scudding dark clouds had been carried away by that high, silent wind. The stars were out around a three-quarters yellow moon. It was a warm night.

Evelyn halted half way over to the barn, turned and gazed up at Henry. "Winchesters?" she said. "Why Winchesters? I told him—Marci's alone up there with . . .Sam."

Henry took her arm and steered her along saying quietly, "Doesn't mean anythin', ma'm. Just a precaution, is all. We always ride with saddle-guns. Anyway, don't you fret. We'll be along."

27

She stopped again, down near the barn. "I don't want to go back up there. I don't want to have to look at—"

"Well now, sure not, Miss Evelyn," crooned Henry, looking back where Langston was striding across from the house with a pair of booted carbines. "No need anyway. You just guide us close enough an' point out the rest of the way. Then if you like, you can head on home. You'll be safe enough. Of course if you like me or my brother'll go back with you."

Langston rigged out the horses without looking around or speaking. He handed Evelyn up and returned to his own animal. As they were riding out of the yard he looked over at his brother, but still said nothing.

They loped in the direction from which she had come. For two miles of the way the brothers had no difficulty but after that they slowed to Evelyn's gait and let her take them along. She did it silently. So silently in fact that the only audible sound was from their squeaking saddles and the dull scuff of shod hooves passing over flaky soil.

Once she stopped and scanned the skyline, then went on again, bearing straight towards that spot where the brothers had camped. When the white-water showed up close ahead with moonlight dancing over its rushing current, and Evelyn swung towards their former camp spot, Henry raised his brows and Langston looked, but gave no sign he understood.

She rode right up to that little creek-side dogleg of land past the oaks and up to the cottonwoods, then drew rein and pointed. Straight ahead across the creek and up into the trees.

Langston said, squinting ahead, "All right, Miss Evelyn: Now tell me something. How long did it seem young Sam had been hanging up there?"

28

She stared at her mount's ears. "A long time. We . . .cut him down. When he hit the ground he was—stiff."

Langston was pensive. "Last night," he muttered. "I don't understand this. Come on; let's get up there." As he raised the reins Langston gazed over. "Miss Evelyn, if you like you can wait. We'll return, then one of us'll see you home."

She dumbly nodded.

Henry led out to the creek, hooked his reluctant horse, slid down into the icy water to the stirrups and gingerly reined on across. Langston came plodding right behind. Upon the far bank the land lay open for a short distance then lifted gradually in a long roll upwards to where the forest began. Langston rode a short distance, dismounted, jerked forth his Winchester and started on up afoot. Henry let Langston walk ahead. He did not dismount but he lay his carbine across both swells of his saddle and held it there with his right hand.

They passed through the first fringe of forest and on to the second rank of trees, larger and denser, the more they walked through. Langston suddenly halted where an acre clearing glowed with star shine, stood a moment then raised his carbine and hooked ahead with it. The pair of them moved into that small clearing. Where Marci Colburn sat upon a rotten old deadfall pine, there was a tree limb jutting at right angles from a fir tree at her back. She looked up very slowly at the sound and watched the two men come across to her. When Henry stepped down and moved around Langston she pointed to the tall grass without saying a word although in that silvery light she surely had recognized them.

They stepped over and looked down through the grass.

29

Sam Colburn was sixteen years of age the year he died. He was stocky and compact like the rest of the Colburns, but in that ghostly pale light he looked a lot older and a lot taller.

Langston got down upon one knee and leaned upon his carbine. Henry remained standing. The boy was face up, his eyes dryly staring. The expression frozen across his features was unnerving. His tongue protruded, his throat was purple where a hard-twist lariat had dug deep. Henry turned away, crossing over to drop down upon the old log beside Marci. He sat without speaking and so did she. Her eyes were dry and swollen, her lips a slack grey.

Langston arose, paced around the clearing and back again. He regarded that perpendicular fir limb, moved softly in behind the punky deadfall and scuffed through grass until he found what he sought: The knife-cut end of a rangeman's lariat. He held the thing out at arm's length and let it hang straight down while he examined the ground. The rope turned in his hand like a dying snake. He ignored it at first, then slowly lifted his eyes from the ground to watch it. The length of worn old lariat turned slowly to the right as it uncoiled.

Henry said, "Lang; I'll start for home with them. You understand?"

Langston nodded, put the length of lariat into a pocket and watched Henry aid Marci Colburn to her feet. Henry said, "Where's your horse, ma'm?" and she simply gave him a blank look.

"Take her up behind you," Langston said, and stood a moment until they walked off before going on over, picking up the dead youth and going to his own horse with him. He wasted time, plenty of it, permitting the other three to get well ahead before he too rode away from that haunted place.

He made no attempt to catch up, either. When Henry and the girls swung off easterly towards the Hunter place, Langston kept riding slowly on southward in the direction of the Colburn place. He was thankful for the night.

Once, an old wolf skulking along, rose up out of a shallow gully almost underfoot. It was hard to say who was most startled, Langston, his horse, or the old lobo. The horse violently shied from that gamy scent and Langston palmed his six-gun in a blur of movement. But he did not fire. Instead he tracked the wolf as it spun and raced away, content to do no more. He was too close and the night was too still; the sound of that gunshot would travel for miles. Under any other circumstances he would have shot the wolf. Not this time.

He passed along another mile, fished out that sliced piece of hard-twist lariat, held it out and watched which way it uncoiled. To the right; always to the right. He pocketed the thing, released the turk's head of his own lariat and held it out at arm's length. His rope uncoiled to the left. He replaced it and leaned upon the saddle-swells. A right-handed man's lariat uncoiled to the left, always, which meant that whoever had owned the rope which had strangled young Sam Colburn wasn't a right-hander.

He had so inadvertently stumbled on to this that for the duration of the long ride to the Colburn place he thought on it. It was one of those insignificant, minor things a man might go his entire lifetime and never particularly notice. A lariat turned an individual way, depending upon which hand the man who owned it, roped with.

31

He saw the little pinprick of light far ahead and to his left where the Colburn place lay, and watched it come inexorably closer as he approached. Mary Colburn would be worried, he could guess that easily enough, what with both her children out so late. She would be more than worried when he untied the loose swaying thing from behind his cantle in the yard yonder.

He paused to look back and listen for Henry and Marci Colburn. They were coming on at a lope. He reined off to let them go past, then plodded along behind them making no attempt to hurry. He didn't want to be the first one to arrive down there. In fact, if there'd been a decent way to slip up through the darkness over there, put the kid maybe on the stoop and ride off again, he'd gladly have done it.

He stopped to make a smoke which he felt no need for, lit up behind his hat and smoked a moment, then plodded on again. He had his reasons. It was easy to discern the riders up ahead spring down at the barn and head for the house. He counted slowly and got to fifty before he heard the shriek from within the house. He killed the smoke and turned in, riding past the loose animals at the barn, past the henhouse and smokehouse right on up to the rear doorway. There, he dismounted, methodically untied Sam, lifted him gently off, and carried him to the back of the house, and there he stood.

No man alive ever gets used to bringing home to a mother her dead loved ones. No man.

"Henry! Henry, come out here!"

It took a moment. That wailing inside the house was like a steel fingernail going up and down Langston's spine. The door opened. Henry blinked into the out-back darkness.

"Take him," Langston muttered. "I'm no good at this

32

type of thing. You better stay with 'em tonight, too. I'll ride on back. See you tomorrow sometime. Mind his head there; don't bang it on the doorjamb. Mind now."

The minute Henry had the corpse Langston turned his back and moved back out into the velvety blackness. The wailing inside tore at him, deep down. He'd heard it before, but that didn't change a thing.

CHAPTER FIVE

TOM MARKLEY WAS IN BRANNAN'S SALOON when the HH rider said Langston Gunn was outside at the tie rack waiting for him. Markley's initial reaction was to ask the HH man what Gunn wanted, but he didn't because obviously if the cowboy had known he'd have said something.

It was close to midnight. Markley hadn't noticed Gunn in town before. He was therefore certain Gunn had just ridden in, and a man didn't ride that far on a dark, gloomy night just for the hell of it. Markley tossed down his cards, muttered to the men hc'd been playing poker with and left the table.

Markley was a large-boned hard-muscled man with the perpetually flattened lips of a man accustomed to trouble and always expecting it. He'd been behind that nickel badge he wore on the front of his shirt for seven years and the only time he'd ever felt not quite adequate had been during the cowmen-emigrant sniping several years back. His trouble then had been that, although he'd been a rangerider and rangeboss most of his adult lifetime, he still didn't hold with riding roughshod over folks, even damned sod-busters.

But he'd survived all that, somehow, and for several

33

years now things had returned pretty much to normal. He disarmed six or seven drunks a month and broke up perhaps another half dozen brawls; things he knew well how to accomplish, and things for which he'd been constructed; Tom Markley could drop a yearling bull with either hand and he perhaps wasn't the fastest man with a gun around, but between the gun and the badge, he got along right well.

He did not much care for Langston Gunn. He'd never told anyone that, not even Hubert Hathaway when the range war had been in progress, because one thing Tom Markley had learned a long time ago was that when a man kept his mouth closed he rarely got into embarrassing situations.

Tom stood an even six feet and weighed ten pounds shy of two hundred, all bone and muscle. He had brown curly hair and blue eyes. In build and heft Tom and Langston were not too different. Tom had an edge of perhaps five or ten pounds was all.

He left the saloon and stood a moment upon the sidewalk letting his eyes become accustomed to the gloom, then stepped over, down into the dust and walked around where Langston was waiting solemnly, watching him. Mostly, the town was quiet and dark. Brannan's place and one or two other variety houses were alight and noisy, which meant there were a bunch of rangemen in town to let off steam.

"What's on your mind?" Markley asked, coming to a stiff halt and peering closely at Langston, slouching with his back to the rack.

"Murder, I reckon," drawled Langston, gazing out at Markley. He didn't like or dislike the lawman. As sheriffs went Markley seemed efficient enough. But it lingered in Langston's mind that whenever Hathaway

34

had ridden to one of the settler's places, Markley had always been in tow like a dog on a leash.

"At least I think it's murder, Sheriff. Young Sam Colburn. Evelyn Hunter and Sam's sister were riding up near the timber beyond the white-water creek, westerly on HH land. They found him hanging to a limb up there."

Markley neither moved nor spoke. He simply stared hard at Langston. Behind them, three cowboys pushed on out of the saloon laughing. They turned to walk northward towards another lighted saloon, their noise drifting back to the pair of tall men at the hitch rack.

"There's a little jog in the creek with some cottonwoods growing there. Due north up about maybe a hundred yards lies a little clearing of maybe an acre in size. That's where the kid was killed."

Markley said, "Is that a fact? How did you find him?"

"I told you. The girls were out riding and found him. Miss Evelyn came down across our range. We saw her and went out. She told us. She led us back up there."

"I see. And where is Sam now?'"

"I took him to the Colburn place. My brother's staying the night with the women. I didn't go inside, but I heard Mary Colburn scream when they told her."

Markley slumped, looked around and back again. He seemed at a loss. He reached up, lifted his hat, ran bent fingers through his curly hair and resettled the hat. "Murder . . ." he murmured. "Who'd murder a kid? Sam . . .hell, Gunn; Sam was only sixteen years old."

"I know." Langston fished in his pocket, brought forth the tag end of someone's lariat, held it out and wordlessly watched it unwind to the right, then handed it to Tom Markley. "This is what they hung him with—whoever

35

did it. I reckon the rest of it's still up there. Also, I didn't find it—didn't look for it—but Evelyn Hunter said the kid's rifle was busted over a boulder up there."

Markley took the rope and scowled at it. It had the look of a lariat which had seen plenty of hard use. He slowly balled the thing in his big hand. "You get a good look at the kid, Gunn?"

"I just told you, Sheriff ; I toted the kid home."

"Yeah. Well; how long had he been dead?"

Langston drew upright off the rack. "Maybe a day. Maybe a little longer. Evelyn said he was stiff when they cut him down. He wasn't very stiff when I tied him over my saddle, Markley, but by then he'd have been loosening anyway, if he'd been dead that long."

Markley nodded, puzzled and disturbed. He rallied and said, "I'm obliged for you ridin' all the way in tonight. Care for a drink—I'll buy?"

Langston turned and untied the nearest horse as he said, "No thanks. There's one thing you could do for me though, if you were of a mind to." He toed in and sprang up. "Let me know what you find out."

Markley said, "Yeah, sure, Gunn; and thanks again."

Langston reined half around, pointed his horse away from town and rode off. Sheriff Markley stood gazing after him.

It was a long ride. Langston did not arrive back at the home place until the small hours of the morning. After putting up his horse he went inside, lit the kitchen lamp, made himself some supper—or an early breakfast—ate slowly, and afterwards drank a second cup of coffee, thinking.

His thoughts were the kind of dead, dull, resisting notions a troubled man had. For three years there had been peace on the range. Whoever had killed the Colburn boy was a rangerider. Even at marking time not all the settlers carried ropes, but all cowmen did. Furthermore, the murder had taken place on HH range, and in the feud a few years back Bert Hathaway had been leader of the rangemen. There was bound to be some talk; some suspicion that the rangemen had committed that murder.

And who could say, for a fact, that they hadn't? It wasn't a settler's way, to string anyone up. Settlers used guns and maybe torches, but they didn't think in terms of hard-twist lariats.

But, Langston said to himself as he finished the coffee and bent to making a smoke, if it had been the rangemen, why would they be so senseless as to make such a glaring point of this cruel murder? It seemed unlikely that men who'd take sufficient time to string someone up, wouldn't also consider the aftermath of such an action. Not only would the settlers get up in arms again, but murder was murder and the law couldn't overlook it, even if the law wanted to. Not any more; not with as many emigrants in the Tanawha country as rangemen.

Finally; why young Sam Colburn? Why not someone like Langston or Henry Gunn who had a good slice of valuable land with plenty of water, whose loss would harm the settlers and would help the rangemen? Why a kid out buck hunting who had nothing but an old horse and a long-barreled rifle?

Langston cleaned up his dishes, tossed his cigarette into the firebox of the stove, closed the damper and went outside to sit a while, because he was not the least bit sleepy.

Maybe the kid had seen something up there, or

37

maybe it had been some of those damned sulking redskins. He leaned against the front of the house watching the lowering moon glide away towards the peaks. Not Indians; they wouldn't have used a lariat. They likely wouldn't even have such an implement of the cowman's trade with them, but even if they'd had one, they wouldn't have used it on a boy. Indians considered being hanged the worst possible death: a hanged man lost his spirit and spent Eternity wandering through the dark seeking it.

He stood out there worrying at his private puzzle totally unmoving as though no single muscle were alive. His body blending to the night, his rawboned lanky shape all planes and angles. There were two things he must do. One was go back up there and hunt for that broken rifle. The other was ride to HH and talk with Hathaway. He didn't like either prospect but he liked less what very likely would erupt out of this senseless crime unless some move was made soon to head it off. By tomorrow night every ranch and settler-home would surely know.

He returned to the house, left a note for Henry, then went out to catch a fresh horse, saddle up and ride out again. It was too close to daylight for sleep anyway, even if he'd been tired, which he wasn't.

Long before he reached the white-water that other puzzle tantalized him. How had it happened that neither he nor Henry had seen or heard a thing, the previous night; they'd been lying there in the bend of the creek, perhaps at the time young Sam was being hanged. Neither of them was that sound a sleeper.

He watched the eastern sky a moment to guess the hour, then considered the nearby brawling creek. There was a ford farther west and he was in no great hurry, so he rode on up and crossed there, then swung back and plodded along beside the first fringe of trees.

The usual little pre-dawn bite was in the air. He had a jumper tied aft of the cantle but didn't bother with it. The chill wouldn't last. Not with the sun beginning to tint the distant skyline faintly with gold.

He found the trail they'd used earlier and went up it into the clearing. It was darker here than anywhere else now. He dismounted, left his horse in the trees and stepped lightly ahead.

Where the forest resumed, northward of the clearing, ranks of trees marched straight on up a rather steep slope towards distant timberline, beyond which no trees grew and bone-bare weathered granite thrust sharp snags towards the paling sky.

Westward, the forest ran itself out, several miles off where a burn had ravaged it many years earlier. Eastward, the foothills swung back, leaving more open land. The pines eventually gave way to oaks and other lowland growth, until they bent far around northward.

It was these hills that gave the big valley its name. Tanawha. There were a dozen different notions what the name meant; even the Indians weren't clear about it.

He took his time. Dawn's brightness wouldn't strike into the little clearing for another long hour. He studied the limb where Sam had been hanging. He also studied the loamy soil around the old deadfall. There were plenty of shod horse marks and no two of them seemed to go or come in the same direction.

Somewhere off through the trees there was a trail. He'd never seen it but other sod-busters had, while hunting the alien slopes. Rumor had it that this trail wound around through secret places and fetched up in a large uplands meadow used by the Indians in decades past to escape the lowland summertime heat.

He returned to the deadfall, sat down, and considered the affair from an aggressive viewpoint. Someone, either up in the mountains or down upon some ranch, knew a left-handed cowboy capable of cold-blooded murder. Maybe he and Henry could prowl these hills for that uplands trail, and follow it to where the redskins holed up. If any of them had done it the others would know; if no Indian was responsible, but there were strangers—murderers—in the hills, they'd also know that.

As for the other route he could take, old Hathaway would hold the key there, more than likely. He'd not only know where a left-handed rider was, or he could find out. And most important, he could—if he would—pass the word that until the Colburn lad's murder was solved, no rangemen should go around any settlers.

A diffused cathedral-like soft glow came into the clearing. He gazed across and saw a half-domed old smooth-worn silvery boulder. At its base lay the parts of what had once been a rifle. He got up and walked over there.

The musket was broken at the breech. Its stock was hopelessly smashed, and even the forged steel trigger guard, and trigger as well as the hammer, had been torn off by the force of a furious blow.

The rock had a pale long scar where the rifle had struck. Someone had swung the boy's old hunting rifle over his head. He had been a powerful man to so completely ruin a gun like that. Powerful and perhaps very angry.

Langston knelt. One set of flat-heeled bootprints

showed faintly. Where the man had taken one forward step to pivot and walk back across the clearing, he had stepped upon the trigger guard. Langston squatted a long time gazing at that before he reached over, dug the guard loose, carried it out some little distance, dropped it and stepped upon it himself, then stepped off. The ground was the same but with all his weight, the guard hadn't sunk more than an inch. He picked it up, returned, and placed it exactly as it had been when he'd first found it, then made a cigarette for breakfast as the sun jumped out of the east flooding the southward range with rich, golden brightness.

He was left-handed and he was a heavy man—heavy enough to drive the trigger guard deep down when he stepped upon it with one foot. And powerful. Strong enough to completely shatter a rifle over a rock.

Langston lit up, strolled on back to the deadfall and sat down again to slowly smoke and speculate.

CHAPTER SIX

AN HOUR LATER when he was stepping off some tracks, he caught sight of oncoming horsemen loping up from the south. He stood just inside the trees and watched. They were coming from the wrong direction to be Markley and some possemen from Minton. Neither were they coming from the west, which meant they weren't HH riders.

He made out old Mike Hunter, Evelyn's father, out where the horsemen slowed. The others were also settlers, five more of them, all armed with carbines and rifles as well as six-guns. He stepped forth and let them see him. At once they bunched up. He could guess about

41

what they were saying. It was still too far for them to recognize him. They continued to approach. He looked for his brother but Henry wasn't there.

Mike Hunter was a glum man in his sixties with a mane of grizzled, kinky hair, and unsmiling mouth and pale blue eyes that viewed life with strong suspicion. He was a taciturn man. He was tall and gaunt. When he eventually got close enough he continued to regard Langston Gunn with the same strong suspicion as before.

The others were motley, mostly gnarled farmers as foreign to the Arizona environment as could be imagined. They seemed relieved that it was Langston, awaiting them up in the trees, and eased off from their former awkward stiffness.

He nodded and they nodded back. Old Hunter dismounted with a rifle in the bend of his left arm. He faced Langston a moment in silence, studying him, then stalked forward.

"Is this the place?" he demanded.

Langston nodded without answering. He turned and led them back up to the clearing where they stood uncomfortably looking from the hang tree to the smashed rifle in the trampled grass.

Hunter remained with Langston as the others moved out left and right. "Find anything?" he inquired.

Langston evaded Hunter's meaning by pointing. "There's the kid's weapon and yonder's the tree. Last night I rode into Minton and gave Tom Markley a shank of the rope that was used."

"How about tracks?" Hunter growled. "My girl said they saw tracks before sunset, back by that dogleg in the creek."

Langston hung fire over a prompt answer. Those tracks

42

across the white-water were his and Henry's tracks. He said, "Look around. There are tracks all over the place. Miss Evelyn an' Miss Marci made some. Sam's horse undoubtedly made some, and when Henry and I rode up here last night, we left tracks. I think what you men might hunt out is tracks coming to this place and afterwards leaving it, perhaps up through the forest."

"Injuns," Hunter growled in a low voice. "Damned lousy redskins."

Langston bent, plucked a long grass stem and popped it between his teeth before he commented about that. "I don't think so," he murmured. "Indians don't hang folks an' they aren't likely to have a hard-twist lariat with them when they're hunting."

Hunter turned his head. "Then who, Langston? The lad didn't hang himself."

Over by the rock where the smashed gun lay, the others were milling and softly speaking, their voices making a soft hum in the clearing's quiet hush.

"I don't know, Mike," Langston replied. "I've been up here since before dawn trying to puzzle this out."

"I'll tell you who," growled the older man. "HH."

Langston said, "Why? The feuding's over, Mike. It's been over for nigh three years. Besides, even if it wasn't, why a sixteen-year-old kid hunting deer with an old musket?"

"Because he's a squatter, that's why, kid or no kid."

Langston said, starting to move off, "I think you know better'n that." He went across to his horse, untied it and paced back again before mounting up. He and Evelyn's father looked straight at one another. Langston dragged his mount around, stepped up and leaned forward from the saddle to quietly say, "Don't stir them up, Mike. Things are bad enough without that.

43

Let's be damned certain first."

Hunter grounded his rifle and leaned upon it. "How?" he demanded.

Langston reared back and gestured around. "Look the place over. Find the tracks where men came into the spot and afterwards rode out again. Backtrack."

"All right, Langston, we'll do that. An' suppose these tracks lead us to HH, or one of the cow camps; then what?"

"Then we'll talk again," said Langston, and started on down the draw back towards open range.

He didn't glance back, and when he hit open country he had to tip down his hat brim; the sunlight out there was as bright as fresh lightning.

He rode at a loose lope, bearing southwesterly towards the more rolling, grassy country. Hathaway's home place was in that direction but he never reached it. He didn't have to. He was three miles down country when he saw the band of horsemen sweeping up towards him. They were riding fast.

He halted, both curious and wary, until he could make out the big handsome chestnut horse with the rusty mane and tail old Hathaway had been riding when he'd last talked with the Gunn brothers.

Langston waited. The others had seen him and were heading arrow straight for the spot where he sat. When they loped up Bert Hathaway's mahogany features were a dead give-away. The older man was hard-eyed and tight-lipped. He knew.

Langston nodded, placed both hands atop the horn and gazed from Hathaway to Charley Bevin, the HH rangeboss, and at the other men, all Hathaway riders. "I reckon from the looks on your faces, you've already heard," he said, returning his gaze to Hathaway

44

himself.

"We've heard," the older man stated. "Markley sent us word last night—or maybe I should say this morning. Gunn; who would've done it?"

Langston, considering those hard, tough faces, became satisfied that, whoever had done it, none of these men was involved. They were hard as stone and fearless men, but not murderers. "I don't know, Mister Hathaway, but I don't think it'd be wise for you to ride up there right now. Mike Hunter and five other settlers are up there."

"It's my land, Gunn."

"No one's denying that," retorted Langston. "But what's the point in aggravating things? Those men are mad and they're not likely to be very rational for a while yet. Sam was sixteen years old. It's different than it was a while back when we were enemies, Mister Hathaway. Then, it was man against man. Now—well—they're pretty upset. You ride up there with your crew and someone might get shot. You don't want that any more than I do. This thing's got to be handled differently or hell's going to bust loose all over again—for nothing."

Charley Bevin, unshaven as usual and hard-eyed, raised his brows. "Nothing . . . ?" he murmured.

"You know what I mean," exclaimed Langston, looking straight at Bevin. "There's no cause for another range war. The kid is dead and whoever killed him is runnin' loose. But I don't believe it was HH. I'm not convinced it was *any* cowman. So, why ride up there and risk gettin' someone killed, for nothing?"

Hathaway listened and nodded and finally said in a softer tone, "I guess you're right at that, Gunn. For a while maybe the riders ought to stay clear of the settlers."

Langston nodded. He had no affection for this grizzled old cowman with his gun-handy riders, but it took a cowman to know a cowman, and he was certain Hathaway would never countenance the murder of anyone, let alone a young boy, so he said, "Send your men back, Mister Hathaway, and take a little ride with me."

Charley Bevin's quick, dark eyes swung. He almost said something to Hathaway but in the end he was silent. The other rangeriders also seemed suddenly suspicious of Langston and his intentions, but they were also quiet.

Hathaway considered, gazing straight ahead. Finally, he jerked his head. "Head on back, Charley. Keep the boys off the east range until I get back. There's plenty of work without coming over here."

Bevin still looked disapproving when he turned his horse and growled at the others. They loped away, back down country, leaving Hubert Hathaway and Langston Gunn sitting there. Their echoing hoof rolls were diminishing when the cattleman said, "All right, Langston; what's on your mind?"

Langston told him candidly. "A big man; bigger than you or me and weighing a sight more, who wears flat-heeled freighter boots and is left-handed, Mister Hathaway."

For a long moment the cowman stared. "You *did* find something, didn't you?" he asked.

"Hardly enough to tell Tom Markley, Mister Hathaway, but enough to convince me the description I just gave you fits the feller who broke the kid's gun and had a hand in hanging him."

"I see. A rangeman?"

46

Langston shrugged. "I'd guess he was. Settlers don't often pack hard-twist ropes. Neither do Indians. The boot tracks have me puzzled. Still, every now and then you see a cowboy wearing those flat-heeled boots."

Hathaway slouched forward and squinted. "I see," he muttered. "I'm beginning to see. You figure sooner or later the others are going to come onto this too, and want some rangerider's scalp."

"*Any* rangerider's scalp, Mister Hathaway. It's going to be up to you to prevent another range war—only this time with the sod-busters doing the attacking. It's bad enough to kill grown men, but a kid . . .I have a hunch even some of the cowmen aren't going to like that."

Hathaway said, "You're making sense." Then he said, "I don't know a rider like you described. But I'm going to find out if there is such a man." He frowned. "Where'll you be tonight?"

"Home."

"All right. Don't leave. I'll hunt you up tonight after I've asked around." Hathaway kneed his horse closer. He shoved out his hand and looked Langston straight in the eye. They shook without a word and Hathaway spun and loped after his riders.

Langston rode in the opposite direction. He heard nothing and saw nothing for a long while, and even if he had, it wouldn't have registered with him right off because he was deep in thought.

But a lone rider crossed his path and hailed him two miles eastward. It was Sheriff Markley. He asked directions and Langston gave them. Markley then said he'd sent word to Snowflake, the nearest town which had a doctor, that he needed a medical man. "For an autopsy on the kid," he explained.

Langston sat there considering Markley. "You sent

47

that word this morning?" he inquired, and when Markley nodded, Langston said, a thin edge coming into his voice. "Why not last night, Sheriff: why didn't you send word up to Snowflake the same time you sent a rider to Hathaway?"

Tom Markley got the innuendo and reddened. "I know my job," he said stiffly. "I sent Bert word to keep clear of settlers. I also sent word why he should keep his men off the west range—because of the boy's murder. Are you tryin' to make something out of that?"

"No," said Langston. "If that's why you did it."

"What d'you mean—if that's why I did it, Gunn?"

But Langston wasn't going to be drawn into an argument with no better grounds for it than he had, so he simply shook his head at the sheriff. "Forget it, Markley, I've already talked with Hathaway. As for the settlers—there are six of them including Mike Hunter up where the lad was killed. They'll be glad to see you—I guess. As for that autopsy—can you hold it in Minton?"'

"Of course. That's where I figured to hold it."

"Good. It'd be hard on the Colburn womanfolk if some stranger rode down to their claim and examined Sam."

"Gunn, I know my job. I've already explained that to you."

Langston lifted his reins and rode on. He didn't turn but he could feel Markley's hostility for a hundred yards after they parted, following him across the warming rangeland.

By the time he arrived at the home place Henry was there. He saw smoke trickling from the chimney while still a long way out and was hungry before he even rode into the yard, off-saddled, and turned his horse into the corral.

Henry came to the door and waved. Langston gravely waved back. He knew what was coming and didn't relish it. Henry had spent a bad night down there with Mary and Marci Colburn.

He went to the trough, sluiced off and hiked ahead to the house. Half way over the yard he picked up the good fragrance of frying spuds and meat. It lifted his spirit somewhat.

Henry didn't give him a chance to get inside before he began. "Hell of a time," he said, leading the way through to the kitchen. "I'd rather take a good hidin' than ever have to go through with anythin' like that again."

Langston tossed his hat aside, went to the stove, sniffed and reached for the coffee pot and a nearby cup. "Did they lay him out?"

"Yeah. My gawd Lang, it tears you apart."

The coffee was bitter and black. "I know, Henry. I've been through that, takin' the dead to their families. It makes a man feel futile, if anything ever can." He sipped crossed to the table and dropped down. "Markley sent for a medic to come make an autopsy on Sam. They'll fetch him to town for that."

Henry's eyes widened. "Autopsy? What for, his tongue's purple because he strangled. What more does Markley have to know?"

Langston nodded stoveward. "That meat smells cooked to me," he mildly said.

Henry stepped over, looked, then lifted the iron frypan. "Autopsy," he growled. "Of all the damned foolishness . . ."

CHAPTER SEVEN

THE DAY WORE ALONG WITHOUT INCIDENT. Langston slept until mid-afternoon then went with Henry down to work upon the barn. They talked a little, desultorily, piecing together what each of them knew or thought, or shrewdly surmised. Once, they saw a solitary horseman pass along eastward, far above their claim. Langston said he thought it might be Tom Markley, and for a while he stood down there watching.

It was nearly four o'clock when Mike Hunter rode into the yard. He was on his way home, he told them. All the other settlers had left earlier and had gone straight south, but he'd angled over to speak a little about something they'd discovered up there.

Henry climbed down to the ground. Young Sam's murder was more important than putting up more siding anyway. Besides, evening would soon drop down over the world. "Come up to the house," he said to Hunter. "We'll have a cup of java."

Hunter shook his head. He looked soberly from Henry to Langston. "Where that dogleg bend lies, on the south side of the white-water creek, we found where two men'd camped."

Henry looked up quickly and might have spoken, but Hunter resumed, his pale eyes unyielding, his down drooping acid lips set in their bitter-bleak fashion. Langston glanced at his brother but only for a second before watching Hunter again.

"The tracks came up from the south, boys, from on down the range somewhere. I don't know where they went but we hope to pick 'em up come daylight and run them down."

"Not much chance," murmured Langston. "Not with cattle all over the range this time o' year."

Hunter agreed with that by nodding. "But we got to try, you see, because them same tracks was up in the soft earth near the hang tree, so we surely got to try. Some of the others aren't convinced, but I am. Those two are the murderers. I'd bet money on it."

Henry went back to the scaffold, hooked both arms over a stringer and leaned there gazing up at Hunter. Langston didn't move. He said, "Mike; did you men see Tom Markley?"

"We saw him all right," mumbled the older man, dropping his brows. "He rode up there mad about something and commenced raising Cain with us for making more tracks. He left a couple hours ahead of us on his way back to town." Hunter rubbed his jaw, squinted at the reddening, low sun, and kicked his horse. As the beast sluggishly moved he said, "Langston; if you boys come up with anything you'll let us know."

Langston nodded and waited until Hunter was well away before wiping his palms and walking over to the scaffolding. "I figured that might happen," he said. "Henry; we were up there when they hanged Sam. How come us not to hear?"

"That doesn't worry me all of a sudden," Henry retorted, "near as much as Hunter thinkin' we're the killers."

"Naw. He doesn't know we were camped at the dogleg. As for the tracks; they'll lose them the first time they run into a bunch of cattle tracks. That doesn't bother me much, but I've been puzzlin' over that other thing since last night. Sam's legs weren't bound so he'd have kicked. His horse should've smelled our animals and come down to them. There

51

should have been the scent of the killers' mounts to make our animals nicker. And—there we lay . . ."

Henry knitted his brows and stared hard at the ground. "Lang," he said after a while. "The way you make this out doesn't make sense. We'd have heard. It wasn't that far off." He lifted his head and turned it slowly. Through the quickening dusk came the steady sound of a walking horse heading straight for their ranch from the west.

"Hathaway," murmured Langston. "He was to come over this evening. I didn't tell you, but he might have something we could use about that left-handed man."

Henry stepped away and said he'd go light the lamp and put on a fresh pot of coffee. Langston stood out there waiting.

The evening was pleasant with a warm low breeze rustling the earth from the south. Their corralled animals nickered; it was near chore time. Langston strode to the front of the barn, took down a hayfork and started forking feed. He'd at least have that much finished when Hathaway rode in. Over at the house light steadily brightened, burning brighter and hotter as the lamp wick heated up.

Langston finished feeding, hung up the hay fork and stepped out into the lowering dusk. That walking horse was crossing towards him. He removed his hat, scratched and replaced the hat, then he stood like stone. It wasn't Bert Hathaway at all, it was Evelyn Hunter. She rode straight up and halted, looked down at him for a moment without a word, then said, "Are we alone, Mister Gunn?"

He was still surprised. In the first place she was the last person he'd expected. In the second place it was rather late for a lone girl to be out riding. And in the third place, over the years, this made exactly the third time she'd ever visited the Gunn place.

"We're alone," he said, "except for my brother. He's over in the house. Get down, ma'm, and I'll care for your—"

"I'll stay up here, Mister Gunn. I just wanted to tell you something. Yesterday before we found Marci's brother, do you have any idea what we'd been doing?"

"Well," he said, mystified both by her words and the way she was looking at him. "Just out ridin' I reckon, ma'm. Springtime's a welcome respite after a long winter, any time."

"You're only partly right, Mister Gunn. Marci and I picked up a set of tracks—two pairs of them heading north. You're partly right; we started out just to ride. Then we began tracking those marks. They were fresh tracks. We trailed them up to the creek where someone had camped. Then we saw where they turned and headed on eastward. But, Mister Gunn, I rode back up to the place where we found Sam today—after the others had gone—and I found those same tracks up there again. That is—I found one set of them."

Langston waited. When she stopped speaking she kept right on gazing at him. It was impossible to tell from her blanked-over expression though, exactly what was in her mind. Then she resumed speaking and spelled it out for him.

"Today, when I rode down to the Colburn place to comfort Marci and her mother, I saw the same tracks again. They went into the yard; one set crossed over and stopped behind the house. Marci told me you'd brought Sam home last night, right up to the back stoop, after I left the pair of you for our place."

"Ma'm," said Langston softly. "I know how all this may look to—"

"Let me finish, Mister Gunn. Those same tracks ended right here in your yard. If you wish, I'll use some matches I've been using and show you those same tracks right now—*over in your corral!*"

Henry poked his head out a kitchen window and called. "Hey; java's hot you fellers."

Evelyn, startled, jerked her right hand from low in her lap. Langston saw the barrel of the gun before he saw its cylinder and hammer. He called out, never taking his eyes off the girl, "We'll be over directly. Keep it hot."

She stared closely at him. "If that was some kind of a signal it won't work because I'm leaving right now."

"For Minton?" he asked quietly.

"Yes." Her voice caught. "Why, Mister Gunn? What had Sam ever done to you?"

"Listen to me," he said earnestly. "We had nothing to do with that killing at all. We were pulling calves. We haven't been home for nearly a month."

"Sure not," she said bitterly. "You two are up to something. Everyone knows the pair of you have been riding the range. But—why? What did Sam catch you two doing? Was it so bad you had to . . .?" She bit the last word off, raised her head, then whirled without another word, hooked her horse hard and raced out of the darkening yard.

Langston stood looking off in the direction of her diminishing hoof-falls and didn't move until a horseman passed around the northern, unfinished side of the barn, halted and stiffly stepped down.

54

"Gunn," Hathaway said, "I thought I just heard someone light out of here like they had a burr under their tail."

From the house Henry called out again, more insistently this time. "Hey; you fellers want some coffee or don't you?"

Hathaway moved over to tie his horse. "That's just fine with me," he said, finished with the horse and stepped over. "Gunn . . .?"

Langston nodded. "Sure," he muttered and led the way across to the house.

Henry had done better than coffee. He had fried meat and bread fried in the meat grease. Hathaway removed his coat and hat, rubbed his hands and took a chair. Henry looked from their guest to his brother. "Took you fellers long enough," he growled.

Langston sat, placed both elbows upon the table and gazed at the cattleman. "Find out anything?" he asked.

Hathaway shook his head. "Not what you're expecting," he replied. "If there's such a man as you figure killed Sam Colburn no one knows him among the ranches. That doesn't mean he's not in town, though." Hathaway leaned back so Henry could slide a dish of hot food in front of him. "There's something else though. Charley and some of my boys found the lad's horse. It was grazing along over on our west range near the burn."

Henry stopped working at the stove to listen. Langston waited for Hathaway to take a drink of coffee. The older man considered the food in front of him then looked around. Henry caught the implication, filled a second plate for his brother, brought a third plate to the table and sat down.

Langston ignored the food. "The horse tell you

55

anything?" he inquired.

Hathaway picked up his utensils and held them, one in each hand, while he looked from Henry to Langston. "Two things, Langston. One; the lad had killed a little forked horn buck. It was still tied behind his cantle when my boys found his horse."

"And the second thing?"

"The boy may have been found hangin' up where you boys found him dead, but he wasn't killed there."

Henry, in the act of spearing a morsel of meat, lowered his fork. Langston gazed straight across the table. "I didn't think so," he murmured. "I didn't think so, Mister Hathaway. Henry and I spent the night just south of that clearing at the creek. We didn't hear anything and neither did our horses. That kid wasn't hung up to that tree until in the morning after we'd pulled out."

Hathaway thought a moment before he said, "Why? Why did they hang him there?" He gestured with his fork. "They had all the mountains and forest to hide his body in."

"To make it easy for him to be found," said Langston. "But tell me one thing before we go into that: Did Bevins backtrack to where he killed the forked horn?"

"Yes," answered Hathaway. "It wasn't a difficult trail, what with deer blood to mark it. He shot the little buck in the burn, which is several miles west of where he was found hangin', an' there were the tracks of riders in the fringe of trees where some mounted men must've heard him shoot and ridden up to watch from back in the trees where he couldn't have seen them."

"Who were they?" Henry asked.

Hathaway shrugged. "Who knows? I can tell you

who they *weren't*—they were not Bevin or any of my riders. I can tell you something else too; they caught the boy up there and one of them hit him one hell of a blow with an oak limb."

Langston drew in a big breath and let it out. He leaned far back eyeing the cowman. "You have that oak club?"

"At the ranch."

"And those tracks—they're not all scuffed up by Bevin and your men?"

Hathaway snorted. "You don't know Charley very well, Langston. He's part Indian. It'd be like sacrilege for Charley to spoil good sign. Why; you want to ride over there?"

"No," stated Langston. "At least not until Tom Markley gets here. That rider who left the yard just before you rode in tonight—that was Evelyn Hunter. She saw my brother's tracks and mine at the creek. She's convinced we killed the lad. She ran off to go get the sheriff."

Henry's lower lip dropped. Hathaway quietly considered Langston for a moment then said, calmly, "Forget it. Tom'll listen to me. If he comes back tonight we'll all of us ride on down to my place an' get an early start with Charley to show us the way. As for that girl—hell—what can a man expect from a female, anyway?"

Hathaway fell to eating. Henry asked a question and Langston explained. What Henry had thought was Hathaway, earlier, was Evelyn Hunter. Henry digested that then asked about the tracks. Langston, picking up his knife and fork, explained that too.

"Yesterday when we saw them out riding, they were tracking us. They didn't know whose tracks

57

they were following. Not until later. And Evelyn got suspicious and did some more sign reading today. This evenin', when she rode in, she had a gun. When she heard Mister Hathaway coming she probably thought it was someone else—maybe an outlaw—and spurred on out of the yard for town." Langston started eating. "Markley should be along directly," he said. "The gait she was traveling and the gait he'll travel to get back out here to nail me, whom he doesn't care one whit for anyway, ought to just about figure out to about ten o'clock, Henry."

It was then seven o'clock.

Hathaway drained his cup and went to the stove for a refill. As he did this he said, "I'll tell you boys what I think. I don't think it was local rangemen or even local townsmen who killed that lad. It was renegades up in the hills, an' they killed him because he either come on to their tracks up there and was actin' curious, or else, where he shot that forked horn, he might have stumbled on to something else. Maybe something they couldn't take any chance of his talking about." He returned to the table, pushed aside his plate and set the coffee cup directly in front of himself. "I have no idea what's going on up there but Charley can find out. He gets along well enough with the scruffy Injuns who spend the summer up in the mountains."

Henry started to roll a smoke. He afterwards tossed down both sack and papers should the other two care to light up. Neither of them did. Hathaway had his java and Langston wasn't in the mood.

"You lost any cattle lately?" he asked the cowman.

Hathaway shook his head. "We always lose a few; poison weeds, wolves, tick fever, one damned thing or another. But if you're thinkin' of rustlers—no. Not that many. And no horses either."

"Hideouts then," muttered Langston. "Renegades on a hot trail hiding out for a while."

"That was Bevin's notion," exclaimed the cowman, raising his cup. "Tom will know if there are any such men in the country. At any rate he ought to know. He's always sayin' he knows his job." Hathaway put the cup down and squinted. "Would you like to know why I think the lad was hung up there to be found? Because someone knows we had trouble once and wants it to start up again. Otherwise, why would his killers draw attention to themselves through the dead boy?"

"No reason I can think of right off hand," assented Langston Gunn. "But who'd want us fighting again?"

Hathaway raised his cup again without replying, and wagged his head.

CHAPTER EIGHT

TOM MARKLEY RODE INTO THE YARD a few minutes after ten o'clock, tied up over by the barn and strode up to the door. When Henry opened it and Markley saw Langston and Bert Hathaway sitting in there quietly smoking, he stood and blinked, then stepped on through and put his back to the door.

Before Markley could speak Hathaway said, "Now you listen to me for a minute, Tom, before you jump off the deep end."

It took more than a minute. It took five minutes just to get it all explained, and after that it required another fifteen minutes while Markley asked questions and got candid answers. Henry went out and brought the lawman back a cup of java which Markley accepted and toyed with, his face puckered into a troubled expression. Finally he drank the java, set the cup aside and shook his head at Hathaway.

"There aren't any reports of outlaws on the run in our territory, Bert. Anyway; what you fellers say doesn't make a whole lot of sense. Why would they hang the kid where a posse might come into the hills and comb them from top to bottom, if they're hiding out. Furthermore; how would they know we'd had trouble here on the range?"

"That's no problem," muttered the old cowman. "We hired extra guns back then, Tom. We fired them when the thing ended. I'm not sayin' those were all upstandin' rangeriders. It could be one or two of them came drifting back with friends."

"All right, Bert. But why? What would renegades gain from the stockmen fighting again?"

Hathaway cocked a jaundiced eye at Sheriff Markley. "Well now that's a foolish question to ask," he said. "They'd stand to gain plenty—cattle, horses, even money, and for every rider or settler they bushwhacked, the other side would get blamed."

Markley pushed off the door, walked to a chair and perched upon the arm of it gazing at the three other men. "Something's wrong," he growled. "I can't put a finger on it, but something doesn't jibe here." He paused to consider Langston a moment. "Evelyn Hunter swears she can show me your tracks—fresh—where the murder took place."

"Sure," Langston agreed. "And I can likewise show you her tracks, her father's tracks, and the shod horse sign of a half dozen other men up there, Sheriff. I'm not trying to talk my way out of

60

anything, but it looks to me like we've got to have a look at that oak club at HH, and also at that spot in the burn where Charley Bevin found bloodstains and horse tracks."

Hathaway got up and struck his thighs. "Get your hats and let's go over to my place. Come dawn we're going to be up in the hills with Charley. Tom; I'll be responsible."

Markley wasn't smiling when they trooped out of the house and headed for the barn. Henry walked with him, behind Bert Hathaway and Langston. When they got to the two tied horses Markley said, "One thing you're overlooking. Evelyn Hunter will tell old Mike. He'll tell everyone else among the sodbusters. If we're not damned careful we're going to find ourselves surrounded by a band of damned irate settlers."

Henry went over to rig out his horse, and also an animal for his brother. Hathaway untied his mount, pulled the reins through his fingers and was thoughtful for a moment before saying, "You're the law, Tom. If necessary you can deputize my riders. I don't figure the settlers want *that* kind of a fight. What d'you think, Langston?"

Henry led a horse over and pushed its reins into his brother's hands. Langston didn't answer Hathaway, he instead stepped over leather and waited for the others to also get mounted. Then he swung and led off riding westerly out of the moon-dappled yard.

Hathaway's remark to Tom Markley made Langston more than ever aware how close real trouble was. Of course the old cowman would reconsider if trouble came; he didn't want it any

61

more than Langston did, but just the way he'd said that, made it clear how easily a range war could break out.

They rode westerly with the warm night around them, with pale light from two-thirds of a lopsided moon brightening their way, and when they saw the brooding mountains, darkly forbidding where trees shut out the light, they were already beginning to drop southward slightly.

None of them spoke even after they slowed to blow their horses, but the glummest of them was Sheriff Markley. It seemed to Langston that Markley must have made some kind of a promise to Evelyn Hunter about arresting the Gunn brothers, and now that he had failed in that, he was glum.

For some reason this thought bothered Langston. It made him turn on Markley with a cold, hard look. But none of the others seemed to notice. Bert Hathaway turned up the collar of his riding coat; the night might be pleasant but he evidently was sensitive to cold.

A light stood up off the distant range after a while, low and squarely burning as though beyond a window sash. Hathaway said one word: 'Home," and led them all closer.

But it still required a half hour to get close enough to make the buildings which were not lighted, along with the one which was lighted. Hathaway raised his head and barked like a dog.

They rode up to the huge old barn, dismounted and walked on where they'd off-saddle and stall their animals. Hathaway was nearest the doorway when a dark, shadowy silhouette moved in among them.

"Charley," Hathaway said, without looking

directly at that shadowy form. "Go fetch that oak club down here for Sheriff Markley to examine."

The shadow faded out. Hathaway finished and led his horse to a stall. "Hay in the far corner," he said to the others. "Whisky up at the main house. Hurry it up, will you?"

They walked out of the barn and met Charley Bevin. He nodded around and handed a sturdy little oaken club to Markley. "That's it," he said. "Take it into the light an' you'll find red-auburn hair embedded in the bark, Sheriff. The feller who swung that thing had a lot of power."

They went across to the main house, entered, waited for Hathaway to turn up some light, then silently passed the length of oak limb around. It was short, not more than eighteen inches long, and swelled at the upper end until it was nearly twice as thick as at the gripping end.

"Regular damned war club," said Hathaway, watching Langston hold the thing next to a lamp and bend over it. "A man wouldn't have to possess a heap of power to kill someone with that thing, would he, Sheriff?"

Markley said, a trifle sharply, "No one's proved that thing killed the kid, Bert. For all any of us know the kid used that thing to finish off his deer."

Langston turned. "Ever see a deer with red-auburn hair, Markley? Look closer here, under the light."

Sheriff Markley did not go forward but Henry and Bert Hathaway did. Langston lifted the embedded hair gently. He handed the club to his brother and faced around.

"Sheriff; what's wrong with it happening like we figured?"

Markley's dour gaze clung to Langston. "Wrong? It doesn't have to be wrong, Gunn. For your sake I hope it's not wrong. But it still doesn't make sense to me, drawing everyone's attention to that murder like that."

"Not even to start the range war all over again?"

"Why?" snapped Markley. "One reason, Gunn: Why does anyone want that thing to bust out all over again? Don't tell me so's they can steal horses or rustle cattle. I can't swallow that for a very simple reason: *They don't have to start a war to steal your livestock!* They can round up all the animals they need and drive them out of the country, and have a couple of days start before most of the open range stockmen would even know they'd been raided."

Langston turned this over in his mind and try as he might to reject it, he could not, in all fairness, do it. He rummaged for his makings and fell to work manufacturing a cigarette. When he finished he handed the sack to Sheriff Markley. "Then come up with something better," he said, holding the match, waiting for Markley to pop the quirley between his lips. "And don't say my brother and I did it, because we had no motive." He held the match. Markley inhaled, nodded, and removed the cigarette to glare at its little smoking glow.

"One thing a lawman learns, Gunn, after he's been at his work long enough, is not to try and force some actual crime to fit his notion of what *might* or *could* have happened. As for some motive you boys might or could have had—I can't come up with one, but all that proves is that you might both be damned clever."

Hathaway, who had left the room moments before,

returned with a bottle and a number of glasses. He lined up the glasses, poured them full, and made a gesture. Henry took a glass, so did Bert Hathaway. But neither Sheriff Markley, who was considering Langston Gunn with an undisguised expression of antagonism, took a glass, nor did Langston.

Hathaway drank, picked up the bottle to refill his glass and said, "Listen you two; it'll be daylight in another couple of hours. Declare a truce until high noon tomorrow and I think we'll have enough answers to satisfy you both. Now I'll go tell Charley Bevin to saddle up, then we can get an early start. Charley'll put us up there in time to see what's to be seen right at sunup."

Hathaway went to the door, opened it, and passed on out into the shadowy night. A draught of gusty wind got inside just before he closed the door, which gave Langston, his brother, and Tom Markley, the first indication they'd had, that a wind had come up.

"With you," Langston said to Markley, "it's a personal thing. All right, Sheriff, have it your way. But don't make the mistake of trying to haul me in until we've let Hathaway's rangeboss show us what he's found."

"I already agreed to that back at your place," exclaimed the lawman.

Henry put aside his glass, picked up a fresh one and pushed it straight at his brother. Langston met his brother's blue gaze and slowly dropped one eyelid, lifted it, and accepted the drink. He had his back to Tom Markley.

Hathaway returned. Their horses were ready and so was Hathaway's rangeboss. Langston tossed off his whisky and trooped out with the others. He paused at the veranda's edge to scan the sky. It was crystal clear, swept clean by the gusty wind. He walked down to the barn with the others, got his jumper off the rear of the saddle, shrugged into it, mounted and rode out of the yard with the others. Charley Bevin up ahead was bundled in a thigh-length smoke-tanned grey coat with red flannel lining. He set his course straight as an arrow for the distant, shrouded mountains and made no change until they were almost to the foothills. Then he swung westerly and made for a great barren scar where a terrible fire had passed through years back destroying everything in its path.

Some underbrush had come back. There were some stirrup-high pines and firs and cedars also growing up out of the char and ash, but for a man on horseback the visibility was unimpaired right on up the slope.

Charley knew the land. He took them along in such a way as to by pass a lot of the choking dark dust, mostly wind-scoured ash. But in watching Bevin, Langston got the distinct impression he was doing this for some different, personal reason, too. He didn't know what, until Charley took them along a buck run back towards the east, and halted to point down where horses had deeply sunk into the layered ash, leaving easily distinguished tracks even in the late night.

"Looks like about five of them to me," Bevin said. "I think maybe the boy saw these marks and started to follow them. Then he stumbled on to that little forked horn." Bevin drew back his hand. "Deer love charcoal. I reckon the boy learnt that when it was too late to do him any good."

Markley, leaning far over, said, "Charley; where do these tracks go?"

"Up where the kid shot the little buck, then over into

the trees." Bevin paused, gazing sardonically over at Markley. "They went through the trees maybe a mile, eastward. They stopped. I know. I tracked 'em on foot readin' the sign. They stopped. I figure them fellers heard the kid shoot."

Markley straightened up and twisted to see Bevin. "And they came back," he murmured. "Is that it, Charley?"

"That's it, Sheriff. Right up to the edge of the forest. Come on; I'll show you where a big feller wearin' flat-heeled boots, sneaked out, got behind the kid and cracked his skull with that oak limb."

CHAPTER NINE

THE SIGN WAS THERE TO BE FAINTLY SEEN but not until the sky brightened to a pale, watery pastel blue could they dismount and readily decipher it.

The boy's tracks were small and spongy in the char. Other tracks sank deeper and were larger. The place where Sam had killed his forked horn was marked with deer hair and frothy blood. Even the knee marks were there where Sam had knelt to bleed out and field dress his buck. Behind them came the flat-heeled bootmarks. Charley Bevin bent to point where the lad's old horse had been standing.

"He got to his feet hoistin' the buck," Charley said, moving his finger along from mark to mark. "He sunk deeper now 'cause he had the deer. There; that's where he heaved the thing across the back of the saddle."

They all saw where flat-heels had glided up and struck. Tom Markley even bent to examine an eighteen-inch indentation. Bevin saw and thinly smiled. "That's where he flung down the oak club I took back to the ranch with me, Sheriff." Charley paused and dropped his arm. "Nice feller, Mister Flat-heels. A tap would've done it. A kid's skull don't take much of a rap to knock 'em out."

Langston and Henry softly paced back around where the flat-heeled tracks went away again, back towards the yonder trees. They followed them over where dawn light was just beginning to dilute the smoky shadows of night. There, they found horse tracks exactly as Charley Bevin had said. They followed them a while then Langston shook his head and halted.

"Right along this deer run, Henry. East. Whoever they were they knew where that little clearing was."

"They'd know," murmured Henry, gazing around through the gloom. "That's a pretty good place to hobble your horse while you're watchin' the southward open country."

The others came along leading their horses, all but Bevin who was astride, leading Langston's and Henry's animals. Bevin cocked a bright, dark eye at Henry. "What's it look like now?" he asked.

"Like the boy made some kind of a mistake and lost his life over it," Henry said, reaching for his reins. "Charley; who'll they be?"

"Strangers," Bevin said at once, bringing Tom Markley's eyes around. "Rangemen—even sod-busters—couldn't spend so much time in the forest as them fellers has, 'thout bein' seen goin' and comin'. On top of that, local fellers'd be missed."

"How much time?" Markley challenged the rangeboss. "What makes you so sure they didn't just ride up in here a day or so back?"

Charley made a mirthless smile at the sheriff. "Get on your horses an' I'll show you why," he said, reined around Bert Hathaway and started walking his horse eastward over the buck trail.

They followed Bert Hathaway's rangeboss for a mile until the buck run lifted to skirt along a piny bluff, and halted where lightning had splintered a tall fir. There was another little clearing there, with an excellent view down both sides of the ridge north and south. Southward, although a watcher would be shielded himself by the lower down treetops, he could, simply by standing up, command a long view of the range for many miles. Bevin halted near the shriven tree and pointed.

"Fire ring," he said. "Men had a camp here. See those dusty places where the grass is flat down?"

"Bedrolls," Bert Hathaway muttered. "How many, Charley?"

"Five. The shattered tree gave them plenty of cookin'-fire wood. From up here no one could sneak on to them. They could see all around. Southward, if you want to trail it out, lies the place where they hung the boy." Charley looked straight at Tom Markley. "My guess is that while you were pokin' around down there, Sheriff, they were sittin' up here quiet as you please, watching."

Langston dismounted and paced around studying the ground. He found flat-heeled boot marks over where the outlaw livestock had been grazed. He returned and mounted up without saying a word. Hathaway, Henry and Charley Bevin eyed Sheriff Markley. Big Tom gazed southward; he knew the country well enough to realize that everything Bevin had said was very likely true. He looped his reins, eased back his hat and let off a rough sigh.

"I don't mind bein' wrong this time," he slowly drawled, not looking at the others for a moment. "But I want someone for that killing. As for the rest of it—there's a sawbones in Minton today an' I sent a wagon out for Sam Colburn, When I get back he'll have the answer about whether the boy was hit with a club first, or hanged first. If he wasn't hit— Charley—that'll shoot your notions full of holes."

Bevin was unrelenting. "He was hit first, Sheriff, you can bet a month's pay on that." Charley looked at Hathaway, waiting. He'd done all he could do. From here on it was up to his employer.

"Go on back," the cowman told him. "And remember, Charley; don't let the men ride the east range where they might bump into settlers." Bevin nodded, lifted his reins and turned his horse. As he was moving off Hathaway said, "Tom; suppose *all* of us head for town and see that sawbones."

They struck out down through the lowland forest where the land dipped towards the fateful little clearing. When they reached it they passed along silent and gloomy.

Out upon the range they turned left, and for the first time they became aware of the warming brightness. It was still very early, not much more than six o'clock.

Markley rode slumped and thoughtful. Henry and Bert Hathaway rode side by side. Langston, back a short distance, saw the oncoming horsemen first and called to the others.

"Riders to the southward."

They all looked, at first feeling no apprehension. There were at least ten of them and sunlight wickedly

70

glittered off armament. It was not difficult to discern even at that distance that the riders were settlers. They didn't ride as rangemen rode, their horses were mostly ungainly brutes, and the men themselves seemed a little stiff and jerky in the saddle.

Tom Markley drew rein and gradually scowled "Posse," he growled. "Who gave them the right; who do they think they are, anyway?"

No one answered him. Langston, drawing up a little, said, "Henry, that's old Mike Hunter out front." He had scarcely got the words out than the horsemen began to fan out and push ahead as though to cut off the riders with Sheriff Markley from either going ahead or retreating. The foremost man raised his rifle without any warning and fired. The range was too great for carbines but that rifle reached them easily. It kicked up a big gobbet of dust and dirt four feet in front of Tom Markley's horse. Tom let off an explosive curse and sprang off his horse on its far side, at the same time yanking forth his carbine.

"Save it," snapped Langston. "You can't reach 'em from here with a Winchester. Get back on your horse and hurry up about it!" Langston was turning his horse as he said that. Henry and Bert Hathaway also wheeled towards the timber. Markley jumped astride as the others hooked their animals and raced northward, which was the only direction open to them. As he hurtled along Markley raised his carbine and fiercely shook it at the pursuing settlers.

"What the hell's wrong with those idiots?" he thundered.

They made it up into the forest with a hundred yards to spare, sprang down and stepped over beside the nearest trees. Far back, the settlers reined down to a flinging halt and came all together out there where they also dismounted.

Langston said, "Keep under cover and don't fire on them." He rapped out that order with the solid sound of authority in his voice. When Tom Markley protested and swore, Langston turned on him. "You do as I say and shut your mouth too!"

Markley sputtered and subsided. Henry called over to his brother. "They think we're outlaws, Lang. What else could it be?"

Langston leaned his carbine against a tree. "I aim to find out." He stepped from behind his tree, removed his hat and flagged with it towards the distant, milling men. They saw him and became instantly still and watchful. Langston stepped farther into view, still waving his hat. To the men behind him he said, "Don't fire. It's probably like Henry says mistaken identity. Hold your fire while I go out where they can see me."

Markley protested again. "Gunn; you fool, if that's Hunter he already thinks you're the one who . . ."

Langston kept on walking, flagging to the bunched up armed crowd southward. When he moved down across the open country he was out of Tom Markley's hearing. Bert Hathaway, stiffly watchful with his Winchester ready to fire, said, "Henry; he shouldn't have tried it. Tom's right. They think you two had a hand in the boy's death."

Henry offered no comment; he was too engrossed in watching his brother's progress.

Then it happened.

Langston was still a long way off but those weren't rangemen armed with saddle guns; they were settlers armed with long-barreled rifles. One of them stepped away from the others, threw up his gun and fired.

72

Langston was hit. He was spun half around before he fell. For a moment the men in the trees were too astonished to move, too horrified. Then Henry dropped to one knee, his face grey, elevated his carbine and would have fired but Tom Markley lunged, knocked the carbine skyward, caught it in his free hand, wrenched it clear and flung it aside. Markley then whirled on Hathaway. "You hold off," he growled. "I don't need bullets from behind too." Hathaway nodded.

Markley stepped out of the trees and trotted straight to where Langston was slowly rising up into a sitting position. He halted, put down his carbine and knelt to look at the wound. Down where the settlers stood, watching, their guns up and ready to fire, someone raised an arm to detain them.

Langston was holding his left arm and gritting his teeth. Blood squeezed through his fingers. "Not bad," he said to Markley. "I reckon the distance fooled him. Just tore the meat a little. Tie it off, Sheriff."

Markley didn't say a word. He removed his neckerchief, made a tourniquet, gave it an extra hard final twist and jumped to his feet, ripped out a fierce expletive and started walking straight down towards the settlers with angry strides.

Langston got up, holding his tourniquet, twisted and called to Hathaway and Henry, who at once came forth and started for him. The three of them came together out there, then also started southward. Where the settlers stood someone recognized the sheriff and called out his name. Markley didn't respond; he thrust along, his arms swinging, big hands balled into fists, and when he came up he still said nothing. He lunged, caught one of the settlers by the shirtfront, knocked his rifle aside and hit the man with a blasting blow that picked up the settler and hurled him ten feet away where he fell in a crumpled heap. Then Markley spoke, his ringing profanity loud enough to carry easily up where Henry and Langston, with Bert Hathaway, started walking southward through the springtime grass.

Mike Hunter was the only settler who faced into the sheriff's fury. He didn't give an inch, but the men with him did, backing off in the face of Markley's wrath, while Hunter said, "How'd we know it was you? We figured it was the Gunn brothers with maybe some of their boy-killin' friends."

Markley turned on Hunter. "Then why didn't you make sure, you damned simpleton? Why didn't you respect Gunn's right when he walked out wavin' his hat? You think the men who killed the Colburn boy are murderers; why damn you bunch of brainless idiots, you're not one bit better!"

"How was we to know who—?"

"Shut your lousy mouth, Hunter," snarled Tom Markley. "One more word an' I'll shut it for you, permanently!"

Mike Hunter closed his mouth and looked over as Langston walked on up, still holding his wounded arm. The men with him looked chagrined and spiritless; they stared at one another or at the ground, their rifles held low. The man Markley had struck, the same one who had shot at Langston Gunn, groaned and twitched where he lay in the grass.

Bert Hathaway venomously said, "You think startin' the feud all over again will catch the lad's killers? It won't. And ridin' my range armed like this could get you all killed, too."

Hunter turned swiftly to reply but Langston reached forth with his good arm and slapped Hunter

74

openhandedly across the face. Hunter staggered, his hand flew up to ward off another blow, he blinked swiftly and faced the Gunn brothers, his eyes bitter and smoldering. "Evelyn told me," he growled. "She told all of us."

Henry stepped over, lay a calloused hand upon Hunter's rifle and slowly wrenched the gun. Hunter hung on. Henry smiled into the older man's eyes and bared his teeth. He had the strength of two men; he kept drawing the gun towards him using just one hand. Hunter's face got red from straining. Then he let go and Henry threw the rifle backwards.

"Evelyn told you, did she," growled Henry. "She told you wrong. All of you." He looked at the others, scorn in his glance like a flag. "Thanks for giving us a chance to explain, neighbors. Thanks a lot. We've just come back from a month of mindin' your cattle for you. Thanks for havin' enough faith in us to let us do your work for you—but not enough to give us a chance to be heard." He stepped back and witheringly looked left and right. The men standing with Mike Hunter stood slumped and crestfallen.

Markley's wrath slowly subsided. He turned to Langston. "Has it quit bleedin'?"

Langston looked at the torn, bloody sleeve and shrugged. "It'll be all right," he said. "Thanks for tying it off."

Markley and Langston Gunn exchanged a look, then the lawman nodded and faced forward again. "Hunter; you're under arrest for attempted murder," he exclaimed. "The rest of you listen to me real good. Neither of the Gunn boys had anything to do with the killin' of young Sam Colburn. We been making damned certain of that since last night. We

75

don't know yet who the men were who did kill the lad, but we know a lot more about them than anyone else does. Now I'm warnin' you—go home and stay there. If I hear of you formin' into another posse and ridin' out, I'll lock every damned one of you up for as long as the law allows. Get on your horses and get out of my sight. *Move!*"

The settlers got mounted. For a moment they looked awkwardly self-conscious, then, without a word they turned and plodded off southward leaving Mike Hunter behind unarmed and grey-faced, along with the unconscious man in the grass.

Henry and Bert Hathaway went back for the horses. Markley readjusted the tourniquet, glared at Hunter, and stepped over to catch hold of the groaning man where he lay. He hauled him ungently to his feet and shook him hard until the settler's eyes flew open. "Get on your horse," Markley snarled, plucking away the man's six-gun. "And don't open your trap until we hit town. You're under arrest for attempted murder."

The settler staggered groggily when Markley gave him a push towards his mount. He threw up both hands and clung to the saddle, his head still full of cobwebs.

When the others returned everyone got astride and started southeastward towards Minton.

CHAPTER TEN

IT WAS A LONG RIDE and during the course of it, as the party passed northward of the Gunn place, Mike Hunter found himself riding stirrup with the man he'd almost gotten killed. He glanced surreptitiously at Langston and just as swiftly dropped his eyes. "It was a fool thing I did," he mumbled. "But, after Evelyn came back from town an' said the sheriff was goin' after you, it looked to me like she had to be right."

Langston said nothing. He'd lost blood, but not enough to cause him any drowsiness. Still; the arm hurt. The more time passed, the more it hurt. He eased off the tourniquet now and then to aid circulation. The torn sleeve was redly plastered to him. There was a gradual swelling too. He tended his injury and ignored the man at his side.

It was close to eight o'clock when they passed the Gunn ranch. It was close to nine when they could distantly make out the dust over Minton. Tom Markley rode along faintly scowling. After a while he said, "The town's sure busy; more than the usual amount of dust."

The others looked but said nothing. They anticipated nothing and were therefore engrossed in other thoughts. Bert Hathaway twisted half around in his saddle to gaze at the elder Gunn.

"You sure figured it right; it damned near came to a war even when we knew it might an' were set to prevent it."

Henry growled back. "There's always got to be a hothead; a damned fool who acts before he thinks. Only, I've always figured, when a man gets up in years, he

77

gets cooler in his thinkin'.''

"Some men," agreed Hathaway, straightening forward again as Markley spoke.

"Riders coming. Looks like they're in a hurry too."

Hathaway swore under his breath and said, "Not again, I hope."

But these horsemen were loping westward from the direction of Minton, and there weren't ten of them, only four or five. As they watched, none of them speaking, Langston slowly drew straight up in his saddle. Henry saw this and anxiously looked from the oncoming men to his brother.

"You figure it's the five we're lookin' for?" he asked.

"I'm thinking something altogether different," Langston replied. He did not elaborate, but kept watching the oncoming horsemen.

When Minton was well in view with its dust and its faint sounds of someone banging on an anvil, Tom Markley said, "Hell; that's Fred Winston and Les Brannan. What's got their dander up, riding like that? Les hasn't been on a horse in five years."

"He shows it," Hathaway dryly commented.

But it was Langston Gunn who made the comment which halted them out there west of town, waiting. He said, "I've got a bad feeling we're about to find out why Sam Colburn was hung where he'd be found."

The riders swerved to intercept Markley and the others. One of them shouted indistinguishably, his words floating ahead, thin-edged with alarm.

"Trouble," murmured Sheriff Markley. "Something's happened in town."

The townsmen whirled up and slammed down to a stiff-legged sliding halt. They were sweaty and pale, their eyes bulging. Without a greeting, or even a glance

78

at the others, one of them, a battered, hatless man with thinning lank hair had a droopy dragoon moustache gasped out, "Tom; the town's been raided while you was gone. They cleaned out my saloon, the general store, and even the safe down in your office. There was five of 'em. They come into town this morning before sunup: They knew exactly what they was doin'. They had the whole thing finished before most folks was even out of bed. Not a shot fired. They was real professionals an' they lit out southward on fresh critters they stole from the liverybarn."

Markley sat there staring. So did the men with him. One of the other townsmen said: "One took the liverybarn and rigged out fresh horses. Another one took one side o' the road, his pardner the other side. Those two had Winchesters. The last two did the plunderin'. I tell you, Sheriff it was about as neat a working crew as I ever saw. Except for the money, there wasn't no hurt."

"Yes there was," said Langston Gunn. "A sixteen-year-old settler kid died to make it work out that way."

The townsmen gazed at Langston, not comprehending, but Sheriff Markley, Bert Hathaway, and Langston's brother understood what he meant. Hathaway slackened in his saddle.

"They had it planned like that all along," he murmured, looking around. "They made sure someone'd find the Colburn lad and drew everyone away from Minton by what they did up there."

For the first time Mike Hunter spoke. His voice was gravelly; he appeared badly shaken. "No; it couldn't be like you fellers are implyin'. What kind of men would deliberately murder a kid to provide themselves with a way to raid a town? You've got to be mistaken."

79

Hunter's words died. Their echo faded. The men sat there gazing at Hunter. Tom Markley finally lifted his rein hand. "Let's go," he mumbled, booting his horse over into a lope straight towards town.

The townsmen rode with them, none of them saying anything, all of them solemnly thoughtful and grave faced. They came close enough to see the excitement which was responsible for all that lifting dust. Horsemen galloped into and out of Minton. When Markley asked about that, one of the others explained.

"We couldn't find you. Someone said you'd headed out for HH. We couldn't wait too long, Tom, or them fellers'd have been out'n the country, so we sent out groups o' riders to scour around lookin' for them."

"Any luck, Les?"'

Dunno; the first bunch that rode out hadn't returned before we lit out westward lookin' for you."

They entered town from the north roadway, still loping. People called out when they recognized the sheriff. Markley looked neither left nor right. Down in front of his jailhouse there was a small mob of armed men in the roadway, some of them holding the reins of their mounts, obviously ready to ride. As Markley swept on up, other men came running from both sides of the road singing out to him. As they were dismounting a shock-headed man pushed through and took Langston by the arm, his face creased into an expression of professional interest.

"Bullet wound," the man said, releasing the tourniquet. "If you'll come with me I'll patch that up for you." The man raised his grey eyes. "In case you're wondering I'm not a veterinarian." He smiled.

Langston turned to walk off with the medical man. Bert Hathaway blocked their way. "Langston; we're going to pick up fresh animals and take the trail. Some of these men say the outlaws were spotted heading southwest an hour or so back."

The crowd was constantly increasing. Men talked loudly and profanely as Sheriff Markley shouldered his way past to enter his office. There was a cordite odor in the atmosphere. Markley came back out into the roadway almost instantly, his eyes fiery.

"Wrecked the jailhouse office," he growled. "Took all my ammunition."

A tall cowboy calmly stood up straight out in the roadway so he could see over the shorter men, and said, "Mister Markley; them fellers are wanted men. I recognized two of 'em. They—"

"Never mind that," Markley barked, looking left and right. "Those of you with horses and guns get astride. The rest of you go on home. They won't likely come back this way but if they do—let them have everything you've got."

He pushed on over where Henry and Bert Hathaway were looking up the left hand sidewalk where Langston and the medical man were walking northward. Hathaway turned to say, "Tom; let's pick up fresh animals at the liverybarn. By that time Langston'll be bandaged up."

Markley considered. "He's lost blood, Bert, and this might be a hard trail. We better not take him along."

Before Hathaway could comment Henry Gunn said, "You'll wait for my brother, Sheriff, or you won't be goin' yourself."

Markley got a dark look across his face. Henry braced into it giving as good as he got. It was Bert Hathaway who finally intervened, saying, "Henry; go hurry that sawbones up. Tom; you come with me to

81

the liverybarn." Hathaway looked around at the other men standing back with their animals. "Get mounted, boys," he sang out, "we're goin' to the liverybarn. You come along." He paused as one man shuffled forward and tapped Markley on the shoulder. It was Mike Hunter. He said: "What about me, Sheriff?"

Markley turned, his smoky gaze steady. "You don't have a horse nor a gun, Hunter, and I don't have time to mess around bookin' you an' lockin' you up. So I'm turnin' you loose on your own recognizance."

Hunter looked blank. "What's that mean?" he asked.

"It means for you to go on home and wait. When I get back I'll send for you—an' you'd better come running. If you make a break for it and I have to hunt you down, there's an awful good chance you may never get to town the second time." Hathaway was impatiently tugging at Markley's sleeve. The riders were already moving up the road in the direction of the liverybarn. Elsewhere, walking men lined both sidewalks and kept up a lively yelling back and forth.

Markley went to the barn with Henry Gunn and Bert Hathaway. The liveryman met them shaking his head. He said the outlaws had taken his fastest horses, but he'd do the best he could. As he walked off Bert went with him. Outside, where the mounted men sat, others rode up to join the posse. Henry glanced anxiously around when someone tapped him thinking it might be Langston. It was Hunter. He said, "Henry; I got to go along. You understand?"

Henry nodded; he understood. "Go get a horse from the liveryman and hurry up about it. And borrow a couple of guns from someone, Mister Hunter."

"Sheriff Markley might order me off."

Henry, seeing Langston coming along from up the

82

plankwalk, said absently, "naw; you tell Markley you got a right to go. Tell him my brother and I said so." Henry worked his way through the noisy throng where Langston was. "You patched up?" he asked, looking at the stiff shreds of shirtsleeve through which showed a clean professional-looking bandage.

Langston nodded. "You better get us a pair of fresh animals, Henry." Then, as Henry turned, he said, "And one more thing—Charley Bevin was right. Sam Colburn's skull was cracked from the blow of a club before he strangled to death at the end of that left-handed lariat."

Henry stopped moving. "The doc tell you that?"

"Yeah. He said Sam strangled to death, but that he probably never felt anything. His skull was cracked too badly. Now go get us a pair of good horses. I want to meet up with Mister Flat-heels."

Order came out of chaos, gradually. The posse men got astride. Tom Markley looked around. He had three times as many volunteers as he needed. He ticked off some names telling some elderly men and some young boys to drop out. When protests rose up he swore at them raising a big clenched fist. The arguments halted. He then split up his large company of riders into three groups, sent one to scour the southward range, another to move eastward in case the information he had about the outlaws running southwesterly was incorrect, and finally, he called on Langston, Henry, Bert Hathaway, and, after a long, cold look, Mike Hunter, to come with him. After that he reined his mount through the crowd and started on down the roadway.

Silence fell, finally. People watched, turning abruptly quiet and grave. Five against five, if Markley's crew met up with the outlaw gang. If such a meeting took place, some of those five might not return; at least not sitting upright in their saddles. Those outlaws had proven themselves very professional. Not just in how they hit a town, but also in how they cold-bloodedly worked up a good enough ruse to draw the law and most of the gun-handy men away from the town they proposed to raid.

Markley's companions were up against as deadly a bunch of murderers as had ever arrived in Arizona Territory. From that kind, there would be no mercy at all.

They left town by the south roadway and turned westerly. The shod horse sign was fresh ahead of them.

CHAPTER ELEVEN

FOR THREE MILES they couldn't make much sense from the tracks. Henry said all those groups riding out from Minton had probably been trailing the outlaws also. But if this completely buried the tracks they particularly wanted, on the other hand it also left an indelible trail where successive parties of horsemen had followed one another over the same route.

They rode fast, that first three miles, but beyond, because midday heat piled up to sweat-out their animals, they had to slacken off. Langston kept even and didn't look much the worse for his wound, except that his torn sleeve stiffly flapped.

Bert Hathaway, for all his years, was spryly alert. He and Henry Gunn rode ahead to make little scouts, now and then. Tom Markley, riding with Hunter and Langston, eventually growled about the outlaws blowing his office safe, stealing his spare ammunition, and leaving his jailhouse in a mess. This appeared to rankle with Markley more even than the fact that those outlaws had outsmarted everyone in the way they'd diverted attention while they hit the town.

Langston said, as they were walking quietly along, that the doctor had explained how young Colburn had died. Markley listened with a long expression. When Langston finished he said, "They didn't have to kill the kid. They could've used him as a hostage. They could even have just kept him hidden until everyone got worried and organized searching parties. That'd have drawn us away from town just as well."

Langston didn't agree, but he didn't say so. Search parties could have seriously impeded the outlaws' plans just by being abroad in the land. He did, however, agree that killing Sam Colburn hadn't been necessary.

It was Hunter who spoke up, saying something the other two hadn't yet mentioned. "Hathaway said he thought at least one or two of those outlaws might have been gunmen the ranchers hired a few years back when we were havin' our trouble. If that's so, why then I figure they killed young Sam hoping it'd start the fightin' all over again. That would've kept folks even more diverted."

Markley gazed darkly at the older man. "You might as well have been workin' with them, too," he growled. "You and those other idiots who shot at us this morning."

Hunter fell silent.

Hathaway and Henry came back from a nearby topout to report they'd spotted a sizeable dust cloud some miles westward. When Markley looked interested, however, Bert said, "It's too many riders; must be some of that bunch from town who went out earlier."

They passed around the base of the hill, and picked up a very faint, dull smash of sound. Langston reined up at once. So did the others. The sound came again, three times.

Markley said: "Gunshots."

They picked up their animals with spurs and set them down into a loose lope, restraining the horses to save them, and in this fashion covering much more ground. A running horse gave out fast, a loping horse could hold his gait for many miles.

The gunshots sounded steadily louder. "Got 'em holed up," exulted Henry, reaching down to un-ship his carbine. "Up ahead there—you can see the sunlight shinin' off metal."

They covered a full mile before they could distantly distinguish men on foot darting back and forth through some dense chaparral at the base of a little knoll with several shaggy old black oaks atop it. Up there, someone spotted their approach and the down-slope gunfire slackened as men cautiously rose up and craned around.

Langston gauged the distance and halted back a short distance, got down and drew out his Winchester. He was beyond range. The others also dismounted and grabbed their saddle-guns. A tall man trotted awkwardly back to them, his face heat-flushed and shiny. The moment he recognized Markley he twisted to point up the hill with his carbine.

"Got one of 'em up there on the knob," he called out. "The others left him."

"Is he hurt?" Markley asked, squinting ahead.

86

The cowboy said, "Well, if he is, Sheriff, he sure don't show no signs of it. He's a reg'lar tiger. We offered to let him walk down peaceable, and he opened up on us."

Langston leaned to hear what the perspiring man had to say. He kept looking up the hill, puzzled. It didn't make sense; one of the renegades up there, unhurt. Why hadn't he kept on with the others?

The cowboy answered that question almost casually. "Around beyond the hills there's a dead horse. He's got a broke leg where he stepped into a prairie dog hole. That feller must've shot him and climbed up there, hopin' maybe we wouldn't spot him." The man turned, wiped off sweat and shook his head. "All we did was stop to blow the horses an' talk, an' he let fly."

"Nervous," opined Bert Hathaway. "Thought you boys'd seen him or something. Well, Tom; let's go get us the first one."

They started moving up, cautiously, once they came into the chaparral, because they were then well into carbine range. Other men converged where Tom Markley stood. There were eight of them.

"Plenty of you for just one man," muttered Markley. "Well; split up. Half of you go around to the other side. We got to keep him plenty busy while someone sneaks up there."

Langston said, "Wait. Did you fellers give him a chance after he opened up on you?"

The men looked at Langston. Clearly, they hadn't, and just as clearly they did not now cotton to any such suggestion. Langston pushed through, walked on up through the brush for several yards, raised his head and called out.

"You up there on the knoll: You got any idea how

many men are around you down here?"

Instead of an answer, the outlaw in among the oaks, fired downhill. The men back with Markley broke and ducked down. Langston tried again.

"All we've got to do is sit down out here and wait. Either you run out of bullets or you get thirsty."

The outlaw's savage voice cried out bitterly. "Then sit down, damn you, an' never mind tryin' to talk me to death!"

"It'd be better if we rushed you," replied Langston. "Or waited until nightfall and set the grass on the slopes afire. That way we can pick you off like a rabbit when you have to run for it."

"Talk," snarled the unseen man. "Mister, you ought to be preacher."

"I'm trying to save your neck."

"I'll worry about my neck. You worry about your own lousy neck, mister."

Langston stood a moment gazing up the hill. In front of him the chaparral was almost a solid, tall wall, as tall almost as a mounted man, and prickly. He turned and went back. Bert Hathaway jerked his head at the others.

"Go on; do like Tom said. Fan out around his knoll and keep a close watch. He's fightin' a losin' war. Sooner or later we'll get him."

As the men turned and started filtering away, Markley said, "He can't surrender, Langston, an' he knows it. After what he's been party to there's no way out for him."

This was the obvious truth. Langston picked up his carbine and started moving southward through the chaparral. Henry and Bert Hathaway trailed along after him. Tom Markley remained where he could bawl orders. He was directly downhill and eastward from the top out, and once, when someone threw a shot up the hill, the outlaw fired down into the brush where the sheriff was. Markley moved off northward a little.

Gradually, as the surround was established, men fired. It was a simple matter for the outlaw to understand that he'd been effectively bottled up, but there'd been nothing he could have done to prevent that anyway; not while he was afoot and his enemies had horses.

He was careful, as the day wore along, and sparing with his bullets. Langston and Henry let Hathaway lead them up through the dense brush to where the slope began to lift off the plain. They were at the southernmost end of the knoll and too close to be able to see up above. Bert paused, shook off sweat and raised his eyebrows. They could leave the chaparral and start climbing. They would be crossing an open space all the way to the top, but until they got up there they couldn't see into the trees any better than their enemy could see over the top out rim and down the slope.

Langston nodded.

Bert pushed on through, studied the slope and started up. Where the other attackers could see him, they paused in their firing. Langston pushed out next, and Henry was the last man. Henry made a frantic signal for the others to resume firing. A long enough silence at the southern end of his hill would make the outlaw suspicious.

Guns erupted again.

The outlaw shot backwards and forwards, never seeming to take very careful aim. He couldn't see the men but there was always their blackpowder, gunsmoke puffs, to aim at.

Langston got up abreast of Hathaway on the left. Henry crawled up on the cowman's right. They pushed along slowly but perseveringly, the uphill rim closer each yard they advanced.

Suddenly, down where Markley was, the gunfire swelled into an almost deafening volley. Someone had unquestionably carried the word around there what was in progress, and Markley decided to cause a diversion. He did. The outlaw ripped out four fast shots.

Langston put out his good right hand with the six-gun in it, touched his brother and shook his head at him. He did this same thing to Bert Hathaway. When those two paused, not comprehending, Langston jumped up into a low crouch and spurted ahead almost up to the place just below the rim where one spindly little sage bush grew. He dropped flat, thrust out his right hand and arm, worked his way up the final fifty feet, then lay flat for a long moment.

Down the hill Henry and Bert Hathaway watched, unmoving. Farther back more men rose up recklessly, their attention fascinatedly fixed upon the place where Langston lay.

Markley's volleys began to dwindle. Langston twisted and made a signal to the men down in the brush. Several of them turned at once and went whipping back around to the front. Two minutes later the deafening gun thunder broke out again climbing steadily until it sounded as though a genuine battle was in progress. That was when Langston crawled his last fifty feet, rolled, got in behind the twelve-inch sage bush, and very gently raised his head.

The outlaw was down on one knee, profiled to Langston. He was savagely answering the volley—firing down the eastward slope and had no time to look elsewhere. He was hatless; the back of his shirt was black with sweat. He was a dark, burly man, not very tall, but thick through like one of the oaks which were now protecting him.

Langston brought up his six-gun, steadied it for a second to take good aim, and fired. The outlaw jumped straight up. When he lit down, his leg gave way. He pitched over losing the Winchester against a tree. Langston cocked his six-gun and pushed up off the ground, aiming.

"Steady," he bellowed over the crash of guns. "Don't try it.

The outlaw lay there grimacing, panting, his right hand hovering inches above his holstered forty-five. Down below men were shouting, the gunfire was diminishing, the sun beat down mercilessly. Someone was yelling: "We got him! We got him!"

It seemed an eternity while Langston stood there with his barrel tipped, and the outlaw with his broken leg tried to find the courage to attempt a draw against that cocked gun looking him straight in the eye.

He couldn't win. At that distance—not more than eighty feet—even a novice gunman couldn't have missed. Langston, from the cut of him, was far from a novice with a six-gun.

Gradually the outlaw's bent fingers straightened, his darkly desperate, unwinking eyes, lost their frantic brightness. He slowly brought his right hand away and reached into the dusty earth to close it into a convulsive fist. A shudder ran up and down his frame. He was in agony. He was also defeated.

Langston moved ahead a foot at a time. Without taking his eyes off the wounded man he called out, "Henry; come on up here and disarm him. He's hit in

91

the leg."

Men yelled exultantly. They started storming recklessly up the slopes still yelling. The outlaw dropped his face into the grass and made a deep-down choking sound of despair.

CHAPTER TWELVE

THAT SWEATY, LONG-LEGGED COWBOY who had first walked back when Markley and his crew had ridden up, identified the wounded renegade.

"His name's Frank something-or-other. I recollect him riding for one of the easterly cow outfits a couple years back when the cattlemen an' squatters was feuding."

They stood around while Tom Markley, who was experienced at it, evidently, cut two straight, small limbs from one of the oaks and lashed one on each side of the outlaw's broken leg.

Henry had the outlaw's six-gun. It had carved walnut stocks with seven notches filed deep into the backstrap, along with the initials F.C.

Langston knelt as Markley worked. "Where did they go?" he inquired. "Who is their leader?"

The oily black eyes flamed with defiance. He was tough and resigned and hating, this one. He wiped his lips with a torn sleeve and lifted his head, turning it from left to right while he gazed at his captors. Contempt was deeply etched in his coarse features.

Langston watched Markley finish up. He worked up a smoke, lit it and stuck the thing between the injured man's lips. "We'll find them, cowboy. We'll get everyone of them. You may even be the lucky one.

At least you're still alive."

The outlaw took down a greedy drag of his smoke and looked Langston straight in the eye. "For how long?" he asked. "This here is a lynch mob if I ever seen one."

"You ought to know about lynch mobs," one of the men growled.

The outlaw looked up quickly, singled out the speaker, stared a moment, then dropped his eyes again, let them rest upon Bert Hathaway and said, "Hell; he was just a sod-buster brat."

Mike Hunter roared out and lunged. Henry caught the older man from behind, holding him in a grip of steel. The others did not react so explosively but their faces showed an almost equal hostility. Hathaway turned away.

Tom Markley said, "Just once more, mister; where did the others go?"

Frank shook his head looking fearlessly upwards.

"Damned if I know, Sheriff. Southward I reckon. We didn't have no special place in mind."

"You're a liar," stated Markley.

The outlaw shrugged, unperturbed. "Have it your way," he said, removed the cigarette, flicked ash and popped the thing back into his mouth.

Standing there wasn't going to accomplish anything; they all came to see that, eventually. Langston caught his brother's eye and jerked his head. Those two pushed through the crowd heading down where the horses were. They didn't quite make it. Bert Hathaway and several others came down off the hill also. Tom Markley called for them to wait, then he too came down. As he was heading for his mount Hathaway asked about the prisoner. Markley's answer was brusque.

"The boys'll take him to town and lock him in the jailhouse."

They were all astride when a number of men came down off the hill, two of them supporting the captive by the shoulders. Some of these men sang out but Sheriff Markley turned them aside by sending them scouring the range in different directions. As he told Henry Gunn: "A light posse travels fastest and scuffs up less dust."

They were beginning to move off when Langston, watching how the others were handling their prisoner, said, "Sheriff; I'll give you two to one odds he never reaches town, or I'll give you five to one that after he reaches town they lynch him before he even sees the inside of your jail."

Markley put a quizzical glance upon Langston without speaking a word.

They rode around the knob and found Frank's dead horse. Sure enough, it had fallen in the heart of a prairie dog village, one leg grotesquely bent.

"Hard bunch," muttered Henry. "The strong survive. Hell; one of them could've taken Frank up behind the cantle."

Tom Markley knew better. "Not the way they figure. These are real professionals. When a man can't keep up, they simply leave him. He knows that's how it's got to be. The same with a gunfight; let one of them get shot up bad, the others walk away and leave him. But there's compensation; when they make a successful raid, this kind, each one gets a fat slice. Hell; without making much of a survey back in town I'd guess they cleaned the place out of around seven, eight thousand bucks. Cut that five ways an' it's more'n any rangerider'd make half

94

his lifetime. So, they take their chances."

Langston cocked an eye at the sun. He had been in the saddle since before sunup with not much rest the day before. It was past noon and the sky was brassy with hot sunlight.

The four sets of horse tracks led steadily westward. They were no longer swinging southward at all. Bert Hathaway who knew every yard of this country for hundreds of miles in every direction, made a smoke with puckered eyes and rode along thinking his private thoughts. Eventually, when they came to the settler country east of HH range, the tracks turned slightly northward, and Hathaway had reason for preoccupation.

"If they keep goin' in this direction," suggested Markley, "they're goin' to cross up about where your home place is, Bert."

Hathaway didn't sound particularly worried but he looked it nonetheless. "Charley and the crew'll be around there some place. Anyway, I don't expect they'll be stoppin'. Not as long as they're within a long day's ride of Minton. They know there are crews out searching."

But the outlaws didn't strike the Hathaway place at all. They instead turned, raced along the fringe of country where the farthest settlers lived making straight for the uplands. Back where they'd originally ridden down from, Tom Markley surmised, and got no argument even from Mike Hunter who grew anxious the moment he saw how the renegades were skirting settler land.

They encountered a band of twelve crestfallen horsemen returning from the west. These men obviously had ridden so fast and so far they'd actually gotten ahead of the outlaws, to the west. When this was pointed out, though, the townsmen shrugged; they'd had all the racing over the countryside they wanted for a while. They were bushed and so were their horses. They struck out for Minton.

It was nearer the foothills that Henry saw more horsemen and pointed them out to the others. The crew was by this time several miles westward of the white-water creek and that little acre meadow where Sam Colburn had been cut down. They were even west of the HH headquarters buildings.

Hubert Hathaway watched the riders Henry pointed out for a moment then said in quiet puzzlement, "What in hell are they doing up here?"

Langston drew rein. The horsemen had also seen Markley's party now, and were halted up there watching. "Your outfit?" Langston asked Hathaway, and got an affirmative nod.

"Charley and the others," Bert stated. "But I told him to keep 'em west and south."

"West," murmured Langston. "You didn't say anything about the south range, Bert. I was right there when you told him."

Hathaway still scowled. "Doesn't make any difference," he grumbled. "He knew what I meant. Besides; there's nothing up here."

Tom Markley lifted his reins and rode on without becoming involved in the mild dispute between Hathaway and Langston. The others joined him. For a half-mile those other riders just watched, then they too began moving out. Where 'the two parties came together was well southward of the nearest shade, and Charley Bevin, gazing at his employer, said, "You fellers give us a little scare. We thought you might be them five renegades."

96

"Four now," stated Tom Markley. "We got one southwest of town."

Bert said, "What you doin' up here, Charley? I meant for you to stay southward where you'd be unlikely to get involved."

Bevin and the silent men with him considered Hathaway impassively. It was evident that the cowboys were going to leave all the conversing to Bevin.

The rangeboss jerked a thumb, saying, "We picked up some fresh tracks an hour or so back, Bert. Got sort of curious and followed them to where they met up with more tracks, and the lot of 'em went up into the hills west of the burn."

Langston's brows gradually fell. "How many?" he asked.

Bevin said, "At first, just two horsemen. Then, later on, six of them. An' I'd say when they hit it up into the mountains they knew where they was goin'."

Langston and Tom Markley exchanged a glance. Markley, fixing Bevin with a close stare, said, "Charley; were all these fellers riding the same direction?"

"No, Sheriff; the first two come upcountry to where they intercepted the other four. It sort of looked to us fellers like maybe they was supposed to do that; was supposed to meet somewhere, then ride on."

"The four men," suggested Bert Hathaway, "would be the outlaws. Who the hell are the other two?"

Mike Hunter had a suggestion. "Friends. Maybe lookouts they had camped separate somewhere. Spies who kept watch while them other fellers rode into town and out again. You heard what folks said in Minton— it was an experienced gang."

Langston's frown dropped lower over his forehead but all he said was, "We're wasting time. Charley;

97

where did the lot of them pass up into the trees?"

Bevin twisted and threw up an arm pointing towards the westward end of the burn where trees grew again. "Right across the char, Langston. That's where we tracked 'em, then saw you fellers and come along the trees to try'n make out who you were."

Langston nodded his head. "Thanks. Bert, Henry, Tom, Mike; let's go." He kicked out his horse and so did the others. The last one of them to lope northwestward was Hathaway; he hung back just long enough to speak swiftly to Bevin.

They passed the place where they had crossed up into the burn four or five hours earlier and rode along the base of the big dark place. Hathaway caught up and, seeing how Langston studied the gloomy place where a segment of forest had been destroyed, muttered: "Injuns. They have a habit, when they leave the mountains in late fall, of starting a few little fires. They say it makes the grass stronger the following year, burns out the underbrush, and brings in more game. It's a damned wonder the fire didn't catch hold down on the plain and burn us all out, but the year they did this we had a week of early rains."

"You caught them at it?" Langston asked, and Hathaway shook his head.

"No. Rain washed out their tracks. I'd have skinned me some redskins if I had. They told me five years later why they did it."

Markley pushed ahead and bent low picking up tracks again. Where they swerved, so did the sheriff. The others, coming up, also swerved up into the forest a few yards west of the burn.

Almost immediately all the brightness dropped away and a silence as old as time itself, engulfed everything.

Because of the spongy needle-layer underfoot, their horses did not make a sound. Also because of the needle-layer, it was almost impossible to do any further tracking.

They halted. Hathaway, who knew these uplands best, grew troubled. "They could go in any direction," he said. "I wish to hell I'd brought Charley along. He can read sign where an Injun'd have trouble with it."

"Well why didn't you?" asked Mike Hunter, a trifle sharply. "You knew we were coming up in here."

Hathaway turned, detecting suspicion and distrust in Hunter's words, but before he could reply Langston swung down and tossed his reins to Hathaway saying, "As long as there's some little thing to go by, maybe I can do some good. At least I've done it before, years back."

They watched as Langston quartered, found a faint scuff on the lee side of a red-barked fir tree, and started off northward. "Stirrup mark," he said, more to himself than to the others, but it was so quiet the others heard him.

Ten yards farther along where a lichen-covered greeny rock jutted through the layers of needles, he found the bright scar where a shod hoof had struck. The others followed on horseback, riding slow and intently watching.

It was painfully slow going; the sign was hard to find and once, where the outlaws had swung west again, Langston lost the trail and didn't pick it up again for a half hour. Markley squinted skyward up through the ragged limbs where the sun was dropping down and assuming a dull orange color.

"Near two o'clock," he said. "Bert; is there some place back here those men'll make camp?"

"Plenty of places," affirmed the rancher. "But which

place? We can go bumping into trees all night and never hit the right spot after it gets too dark to see their trail."

Langston found a bear tree with the shredded bark lying all around and halted there looking ahead. He wasn't sure where the trail went from here and something Hathaway had said made him ponder.

"Wait here," he told them. "No sense in all of us blundering around. Give the horses a rest. I'll scout up ahead and see if I can find anything."

The others, dejected now, heavily swung off and looked around. Langston left them in a loose trot, heading straight west along the gentle slope. He was almost at once lost to sight.

Two encouraging things caught his eye. The first one was sorrel horsehair on a stump where a horse had brushed past, and the second was churned earth where riders had temporarily halted.

But it was the third observation he made which both halted him hard in his tracks and also gave indisputable proof he was on the right track.

A man stepped silently from behind a tree and cocked his gun at Langston.

CHAPTER THIRTEEN

THE STRANGER WAS SOILED, unshaven, and smiling, his small icy eyes as sere and merciless as the eyes of a timber wolf. He said, "Mister; for a feller walkin' along on foot you sure are a long way from home."

Langston stood perfectly still. The way the stranger was holding his Winchester meant business. It crossed his mind that if the outlaw thought he was alone as well as

100

afoot, he might not pull the trigger. The other renegades couldn't be too far ahead. If Langston could prevent the man from firing he'd also prevent the other outlaws from being warned that pursuit was close by. He searched for something to say.

"Picked up some tracks back a ways," Langston said candidly. "Must've been yours, stranger, only it looked like the sign of more'n one man."

The outlaw's lips lifted. "You're pretty cool, mister. An' you think fast, which is good in a man. Only, don't lie to me because I didn't just hatch out either. Where are the others? How far back?"

"What others?" asked Langston, estimating the distance between them and conceding it was too great; one lunge and the renegade could cut him in two with that low held saddle-gun.

"I told you; don't lie to me," replied the outlaw. "One thing I never could stand—liars. Where are the fellers who rode up here with you?"

Langston tried for time. He couldn't be certain this rearguard hadn't already spotted Markley and the others.

"I could ask you the same thing," he murmured, looking around.

The outlaw's smile didn't fade. "Sure you could. But I got the gun—not you—so I ask an' you answer. Now, for the last time; how far back are they an' how many are there?"

Langston had his inadvertent answer; the sentry hadn't seen the others or he wouldn't have asked how many of them there were. He slouched, hooked his thumbs in his gun-belt and looked the stranger right in the eye as he lied to him.

"There aren't any others. I left my horse a half-mile

101

back while I checked out the trail. Seemed curious to me, a bunch of riders comin' up in here. Hell; there's nothing up here but a band or two of redskins after their winter meat."

The outlaw considered Langston thoughtfully for a long time before he said, "Maybe so. Maybe not. But either way we got the whiphand, cowboy." The man shifted position, gripped his Winchester one-handed and reached around into a hip pocket. He drew something out and rolled it up into a ball, tossing it over at Langston's feet. "Pick it up," he ordered. When Langston didn't take his eyes off the gun barrel the outlaw grinned his wolfish smile again. "Don't worry, I'm not baitin' you. Pick it up."

Langston bent, scooped up the ball of cloth and instantly, when his hand closed around it, he caught the fresh scent.

"Unfold it," the outlaw ordered. Langston obeyed. He knew what the thing was even before the renegade told him. "We was comin' upcountry, mister, and run on to these two girls. They're with us now. That there headscarf come off the tallest one. She's a right handsome long-legged big girl with eyes the color of a winter sky."

Langston gazed at the scarf with a sinking heart. This accounted for those two mysterious riders the four fleeing outlaws had encountered, and whom Mike Hunter had thought were more of the same band. If Mike had been there, Langston thought, he'd have died a hundred deaths. The girl this man was describing was Evelyn Hunter!

Langston looked up. "And the other one?" he inquired.

"Shorter, but stacked up like a two-year-old filly

with her mane roached. Reg'lar damned spitfire too. The tall one had to talk to her like an old granny to keep her from doin' somethin' that'd have got her skull crushed."

"What'll you do with them?" Langston asked softly.

The grinning outlaw said, "That's up to you, cowboy." He paused. "I'd say, from the look on your face, that you know them two heifers."

"I know them all right. I know something else, mister; you touch either one of them and if it takes ten years, you'll get tracked down for it."

The outlaw was unperturbed. "Talk," he said. "Cowboy; we don't aim to hurt 'em. Not if you an' anyone else who's bangin' around in these hills, don't push us too hard. All we want is clear passage out of your country."

Langston slowly stuffed the little scarf into his shirt pocket. It was no accident, this man waiting down trail. The renegades had anticipated swift pursuit and had taken this effective means for preventing it from getting any closer. That they would kill Evelyn Hunter and Marci Colburn he never for one moment doubted. All he had to remember to convince himself of this, was young Sam Colburn lying there swollen and purple—and dead.

"Maybe you're what you say, an' maybe you ain't," drawled the renegade. "It don't really matter now, does it? But you'll find other fellers trackin' us, so if you want to see those girls alive again, you just trot on back down to the plain and when the others come ridin' along, you explain to 'em how things are an' how things'll be if anyone crowds us before we get over the hills an' down the far side, out of Tanawha

103

Valley."

"When will you turn the girls loose?" Langston asked.

"When we're couple hundred miles away. Don't worry. We won't touch 'em. All we want is free passage. That's fair enough ain't it?"

"Real fair," responded Langston sarcastically. "Mister; that girl with the shirt-cropped hair—it was her brother you fellers hit over the head and hanged."

The outlaw's small, very pale eyes got still. His smile faded. "So you *are* one of them," he murmured. "You damned near had me convinced you was just some rangerider pokin' around maybe huntin' stray critters."

"No point in playing games now," said Langston crisply. "I'm one of them, and there are a hell of a lot more. If you pull that trigger it may warn your friends, but mister, it'll also warn my friends. And the men with me, waiting back down the trail, know every foot of these mountains."

The outlaw got thoughtful. Eventually he said, "Mexican stand off."

Langston disagreed. "No. You boys have the whip hand. You have Evelyn Hunter and Marci Colburn. There's no stand off because we're not going to cause trouble and maybe get the girls hurt."

"Smart," murmured the renegade, slowly smiling again. "You're right smart, mister. Go on back and show the others that scarf. Tell them that I'll be watchin' the back trail every mile of the way. If I see so much as one man—I'll leave somethin' besides a scarf beside the trail next time. You understand, cowboy?'"

"Yes."

"Good. Because I'm not bluffing. I never bluff. Neither do my friends. That's how the redskins used to stop a chase, mister, and it worked. They'd leave a finger, first. If that wasn't warning enough, next time they left a hand or a foot. If that didn't stop pursuit they left a corpse with its damned throat gashed from ear to ear. You get my point?"

"I said I understood," Langston replied very quietly.

The outlaw flagged to his right with the carbine barrel. "Go on. Go back and tell your friends. Then get out of the mountains. I'll be watchin', cowboy. If I don't see you boys ride out—first it'll be a finger. Now go on."

Langston didn't linger. He turned and walked straight back the way he'd come. Until he knew the trees shielded his back he had a tightness up between the shoulder blades. He didn't really believe the renegade would shoot him in the back, but his conviction was a long way from being a certainty until he got all the way back where the others were waiting, their faces damp and anxiously impatient.

He said, "Get astride, we're heading back down out of here."

Tom Markley's eyebrows shot straight up. Bert Hathaway stood up off a rock he was perching upon. Henry and Mike Hunter were nonplussed. "What're you talkin' about?" Bert demanded. "What'd you find up there?"

Langston went to his horse, looped the reins and stepped up and over leather. "Follow me down out of here," he told them thinly, "and I'll explain as soon as we're out of the trees. Now come along."

The others got astride and, after trading bewildered looks, followed Langston back down through the trees.

Mike Hunter muttered to himself looking dark and thwarted all the way out to the plain. Even there, Langston didn't stop. He rode straight southward which was the surest way he knew to put the five of them out in plain sight. Finally, when they were a mile southward over HH range Tom Markley halted his horse and turned a hard look upon Langston Gunn.

"This," he announced, "is as far as I go. What's wrong with you, Langston?"

Instead of immediately replying, Langston dismounted, ambled over, lay a hand upon Mike Hunter's reins near the bit, fished out that little gossamer scarf and held it up. "Recognize this thing?" he asked Hunter.

The older man frowned and stared—and suddenly let off a hoarse oath. The minute he did that Langston clamped down upon his reins preventing Hunter from hauling back and whirling his mount. In a totally dispassionate voice he explained what had transpired up there in the trees where he'd encountered that outlaw.

The others looked and listened and afterwards twisted to run long, searching glances up the gloomy slopes. Tom Markley slowly faced forward again and gazed at Hunter. All of them did. Hunter reached for the scarf and crumpled it in one work-roughened paw of a hand.

For a long time no one said anything. Langston, still on the ground, still holding Hunter's reins, let the old man slowly come to the hard realization that anything he might now do would definitely put his daughter's life in peril, then Langston relaxed his hold, turned and mounted his animal again.

"Head for town," he said simply. "All but two of

us. Hunter; you ride on down among the settlers. Explain what's happened. Forbid any of them to ride up near the mountains at all. I don't give a damn what they think—tell them not a single person's to go up there. And Mister Hathaway; the same applies to the ranchers."

Hathaway nodded. "I understand," he murmured. "But I promise you one thing; there'll be a day of reckoning for those men."

"Just let Henry and Sheriff Markley and me worry about that," stated Langston, easing out his horse. "And make damned certain no one tries to go after them. *Damned* sure. The chances for those girls isn't too good at best. One slip up and I'm convinced they'll kill them just as off-handedly as they killed young Sam Colburn."

"Don't fret," growled Hathaway. "I'll go personally among the cowmen."

They had ridden another mile towards Minton before Sheriff Markley said, "What's on your mind, Langston?"

"You and Henry and I are going to take the north stage through the mountains into the northward range. We're goin' to hire horses over there and pick up the trail—after those men are certain they're safe and *after* they've released Marci and Miss Evelyn."

For a considerable distance the others turned this proposal over and over without commenting upon it. Once, where they saw a small band of horsemen loping eastward towards town, Hunter muttered something, but it was indistinguishable and the others did not ask him to repeat it.

They saw the buildings firm up off the distant range just before sunset. Behind them where the red

107

disc hung suspended above a northwestward peak, there lay a fierce blaze of late day coloring.

When they were only a half mile out, Sheriff Markley said, "Langston; there's a late stage out. Maybe that'd be the one to take. If we handle it right no one'd see us go."

Hathaway furrowed his brow. "Suppose I come along after I've spread the word to keep clear of the mountains. I know most of that northwest country beyond the—"

"You stay here," Langston ordered. "Someone's got to be handy around Minton who knows what's going on. You and Hunter will likely have your hands full anyway. I've got a feeling it's not going to be so easy, keeping the settlers from streaking it after those men when they find out what's happened."

Markley agreed with that. "I'll deputize you, Bert. You've got the riders to patrol the range with. Hunter? You tell the other squatters the HH men are the law until we get back. And by gawd you make 'em stay in line. There's no need for dissension among us now. If anything, we've got to stand together like we've never stood together before."

Hunter's wan face looked grey from more than just weariness. He dumbly nodded. This had been a terrible day for him right from the start. Once, just as they were entering Minton, he reined over to Langston Gunn and muttered something low which the others missed but to which Langston said, "Forget it. It's done, and anyway maybe I'd have felt the same way."

The minute they entered town and were recognized in the evening glow, men stepped forth to hail them; to call forth questions. Tom Markley acknowledged

108

none of it as he led on down towards his jailhouse. There, the same lank-haired, mustached townsman who'd been among the riders who had ridden out to intercept Markley hours earlier with news of the raid on Minton, rose up off a bench out front with a shotgun in his hands, strolled over and said, "Sheriff; we locked up that feller you brang in. The one who shot Mister Gunn. I reckon, in all the earlier confusion, you forgot him. Well; we locked him up right after you fellers rid out."

Markley dismounted and handed the man his reins. "Take these horses up to the liverybarn, will you?" he said, then moved on across to enter his office.

The others also went into the jailhouse. Outside, a little clutch of people ambled up to linger and talk, but Markley did not come out again.

CHAPTER FOURTEEN

THERE WERE TWO PRISONERS. The wounded outlaw named Frank was in a cell adjoining the dejected sod-buster with the big purple swelling alongside his jaw. Both captives looked up when the Gunn brothers and Tom Markley walked in. They waited, possibly expecting more men to come in out of the roadway. None came, though.

Markley considered the jailed outlaw for a moment before he turned to Langston to say, "What was that bet you offered—two-to-one the boys wouldn't deliver him to Minton alive?"

Langston reached into his right pocket, drew forth a pair of silver cartwheels and placed them upon the desk. "Seein' as how you never took the bet and never put up a dime, I'm giving you the benefit of it. Now then;

somebody's got to go get seats on tonight's stage."

Markley nodded. "I'll go. I need to look the town over anyway," he said, and stepped towards the door.

Langston moved too. "I'll go with you. I'll pay for my fare and my brother's on the northward coach."

Markley shrugged. "Suit yourself," he murmured, opened the door and stepped out into the smoky night. He turned to slowly pace northward.

Langston, still in the doorway, looked over at Frank in his cell, looked over at his brother standing near Markley's desk, and lifted one brow. Henry thought a moment, then gravely nodded his head.

Langston went on out, closed the door after himself and walked on up where Tom Markley was standing in a recessed opening testing a door. It was locked, Tom stepped back out and, seeing Langston watching, said, "You'd be surprised how many merchants head for home forgettin' to lock their stores."

They checked other doors. This was what Markley called "Making his rounds." It took time, but after they'd stopped at the stage office and bought passage for three, northward, Langston didn't mind because there was nothing else to do and anything under those circumstances was better than doing nothing.

They encountered the doctor. Langston had spoken with him earlier but Tom Markley hadn't. The doctor reaffirmed for Markley what he'd earlier explained to Langston about how young Sam Colburn died. The sheriff asked several questions then they walked on.

They were in front of Brannan's saloon when Markley halted and sighed. "A hard and discouragin' day," he said. "How about it?"

Langston held the door, let Markley pass through,

110

then followed him. They got halfway to the crowded bar when men began recognizing them and calling out; they wanted to know what progress had been made in the search for the young settler's killers. Markley waved them off for a while, patiently, but because the room was noisily crowded and they persisted, Markley's patience ran out. After a few very pointed remarks the men left him alone.

They were rangemen. Some had been out with posses during the day. All of them had to some degree been drinking and they knew perfectly well who Langston Gunn was—a settler. Brannan's place was a cattlemen's saloon. There was a little talk here and there. Had Langston been alone or even with another settler, there probably would have been quick trouble. Being with Tom Markley was a deterrent. At least it was a temporary deterrent.

They had two straight shots of rye whisky and smoked, relaxing against the bar near its southward terminus. Markley was moody until after his second drink, then he turned loose and candid.

"I got to admit," he said, "when you ride in with that story of the Colburn kid, I sort of wondered about you maybe somehow having a hand in it."

Langston viewed his tired, beard-stubbled features in the backbar mirror. "I've always had a high regard of you too," he murmured.

They exchanged a glance. Markley shrugged. "During the feuding a few years back—"

"Forget that," stated Langston, interrupting. "Resurrecting all that was said and done then can't possibly help anyone—not now. Care for another drink?"

"No. Two are enough. How come Henry didn't

join us?"

Langston shook his head when the barkeeper came along. The barman went on past and Langston said, "He's getting a little information for us, Sheriff."

"What kind of information?"

"Well; that northward country over the mountains is pretty big. With a lot of luck the outlaws should make it over and down the far side by tomorrow afternoon. But the question is not so much *when* they'll come down, as *where.*"

Very gradually Tom Markley drew back from the bar and gazed at Langston. He didn't say anything though. It was not hard to discern his thoughts though. Langston returned his solemn stare.

"Frank would know, Sheriff, but Frank's tough. We found that out when we caught him atop his hill this afternoon. A lawman couldn't get anything out of him." Langston straightened up as a pair of rough looking cowboys came up. He had just barely time to finish what he had to say before the cowboys barged in. "But Frank'll talk to my brother. I'd bet a month's wages on that."

Whether Markley meant to speak or not, he didn't get the chance. One of those rangeriders fixed Langston with a hard stare and said, "Mister; ain't no sod-busters allowed in Brannan's bar. This here is for cattlemen only."

Tom Markley looked up in surprise. He'd been concentrating on Gunn, had no idea those cowboys were behind him until he turned. The second rider was a solid, red-haired man with reckless lips and bold dark eyes. He had his right hand lightly resting upon his holstered forty-five.

This one said, "Sheriff; you sell out or somethin'

112

runnin' with the likes of this feller? Hell; for all we know he might be one of the lynchers that hung the kid—to stir up trouble. They been stealin' cattle right along, even after the fightin' stopped. I always say once a—"

Markley growled and moved with surprising speed for a large man. He first struck aside the cowboy's gunhand, then he sledged upwards with a punch that traveled no farther than his belt buckle. It caught the red-headed man flush on the chin. His head snapped back, his knees turned loose, and he fell without a word, striking a bystander, bouncing off to hit a card table, and dropping from sight.

"That's enough," someone snarled behind Tom Markley. When he turned he was looking into the barrel of the other cowboy's gun. He teetered a moment, then dropped down flat-footed, raising his angry countenance.

Langston was quartered away from this man enough to conceal his good right arm. His injured left one, with the blood-stiff sleeve, was visible. He was slow to speak, not wishing to divert Markley, but when it became evident the lawman had no intention of jumping the other cowboy, whose gun was rock-steady and whose inflamed eyes did not waver, Langston said, "Maybe you're right at that. Maybe I shouldn't be in here because this is a cowman's saloon. But today I saw a lot of rangemen riding after some murderers who'd killed a settler, not a cowman."

Gradually, the saloon became still. Men craned to see, then sidled clear and kept still. The bartender had one hand atop his bar, one hand below it. He was a battered, stony-faced individual with a cold expression of hostility fixed towards that fired-up rangerider.

Markley said, "Put up that gun."

The cowboy shook his head. "Not by a damned sight. What'd you slug my pardner for?"

"For," growled Tom Markley, "being a damned fool, an' unless you put up that gun you're goin' to get the same."

The cowboy flicked a look at Langston and back again to Sheriff Markley. Langston said, "Mister, look down over here." The cowboy kept warily eyeing Markley. In his hazy mind he understood that, somehow, something had gone wrong here. For one thing the other rangemen in the saloon were keeping clear. For another, he had an angry Sheriff Markley facing him. And finally, his pardner was no longer backing up his play.

Langston spoke again. "I said look down here, cowboy. You're covered."

The rider dropped his eyes once then swiftly lifted them again. Markley too, glanced down. Langston's six-gun was peeping from low on his right side. Others finally saw that gun too. The prudent ones, estimating possible trajectory, tip toed well away.

Langston said, "Put up your gun."

The cowboy's curled knuckles turned white from squeezing his pistol grip. "Try an' make me, sod-buster," he snarled.

Langston had an answer for that, too. "I can do better'n that, cowboy. I can kill you before you even get set."

Langston slowly pushed his right hand out where everyone could see it. His gun was already cocked. The cowboy hadn't cocked his gun, he'd only drawn it. Langston's meaning was very clear.

Tom Markley, dark in the face, glared across the intervening space, saying, "Five seconds, cowboy, then

114

you either pull the trigger and hope you make it—or else."

From farther down the bar a thick-shouldered graying rider stepped back and turned. "Slim," he called quietly. "Do like they're tellin' you: Put up that damned gun. What's got into you anyway? The sheriff's been hard at it, so has that Gunn feller. You're actin' like the range war's still on, and everyone knows it ain't. Now put away that darned gun."

As this man spoke he rolled up past the other men lining the bar to halt beside the cowboy. He was older and scarred and savvy, a good man to have around in any kind of trouble. He mumbled something, put out his hand, took hold of the gun hand and leaned. At once that tipped-up barrel began to droop. As the older man did this he looked at Langston and Markley.

"Slim's all right, fellers," he said calmly. "Just sometimes when he's been drinkin' . . ." The burly man finished forcing the gun down, reached over and pried it out of the cowboy's fingers, stepped back and let off a big breath. Slim stood there grey and uncertain. Tom Markley's savage stare was hard against him. Langston straightened around, eased off his hammer and put up his six-gun. To the cowboy and the older rider who was standing there holding the cowboy's gun, waiting for whatever came next he said, "Care for a drink; or maybe we'd ought to go find us a saloon where they don't care whether a man's cowman or a sod-buster."

The thick-shouldered man answered, eyeing Sheriff Markley askance. "Hell; that's silly stuff, Mister Gunn. A man's a man. Either he's a decent sort or he ain't—and I reckon the cowmen got just as many that

115

ain't as anyone else has." He gave the cowboy a sharp jab with his thumb. "Up to the bar, Slim, Mister Gunn's buyin'."

Tom Markley's big shoulders lost their stiffness. He and Langston exchanged a look as the cowboys moved past. Langston gently wagged his head as though to say since it had ended all right and since the cowboy called Slim had been told off by one of his crew, it should be left like that.

Markley didn't nod agreement and he did not lose his harsh expression, but he did step up to the bar and bang upon it.

They had their drink, the four of them. Elsewhere throughout the big room men went back to whatever they had been doing, but there was not quite so much noise as before, and occasionally heads were turned, eyes rolled half around. These were tough, seasoned rangemen; they knew how quickly such a truce could be dissolved. Only a fool didn't keep a weather eye peeled so as to know which way to leap if it came to that.

But it didn't. The thick-shouldered man amiably thanked Langston for their drinks, gripped Slim by the arm and took him far along toward the north end of the bar. Markley and Langston looked into the back bar mirror. Down there that older man was wrathfully reading the riot act to Slim. Some other cattlemen strolled up and joined in. Slim wilted and hung there against the bar.

Two card players solicitously picked up the unconscious red-head, dragged him by the armpits outside and left him propped against the roadside front wall where the cool night air might aid in his revival. Then they returned, sat down and took up their cards from where they'd hastily dropped them ten minutes

116

earlier and without even looking up, resumed their game.

Markley finally spoke. "I should've locked him up."

Langston said, "Why? That wouldn't have done half as much to him as his husky friend and those others are doing right now."

"You don't understand the law," mumbled Markley, and reared back to take out his pocket watch and gaze at it.

"I understand men," Langston retorted. "What time is it?"

"Time to go. The coach'll be here any minute."

They walked out of the saloon. Several dozen sets of eyes followed them and for a while after they'd departed no one said anything. Then the barman, making a wide swipe of his counter where they'd stood, turned and ran a caustic glance up where Slim and his companions were standing. "Mister," he loudly exclaimed, "that's as near as you're ever goin' to come to gettin' killed. That feller called Gunn comes by his name honestly. He had you covered when you drew. I seen him do it. He was so much faster'n you it was pitiful. Except that he's a pretty decent feller, you'd be turnin' cold by now." The barman finished wiping, hung his bar rag on a nail and went along to where those cowboys stood, reached for their emptied glasses and tapped Slim in the arm "Out. Out, mister, and don't come back. An' as for Les Brannan's place being just for cattlemen; that changed startin' tonight. Sod-busters are welcome here the same as cowmen or anyone else. Only fellers we ain't go to have comin' in here is troublemakers. Now get out and stay out!"

It was quite a sermon but no one challenged it. In fact one rangeman raised a glass. "Fair enough," he said. "Who's with me?"

Other glasses were raised. The men up there with Slim took him and led him outside without a word.

CHAPTER FIFTEEN

HENRY WAS IDLING OVER AT THE STAGE OFFICE. When he saw Tom Markley and his brother coming, he went out under the shadowy overhang to meet them. He had something in one hand which he wordlessly handed Langston. It was a new blue work shirt. Langston took it.

"Obliged," he said. "I'll step around back and put it on."

Markley raised his head, turning as he did so. "No time. Put it on inside the coach. I can hear the thing now."

Henry turned as did Langston. The stage came up through patches of orange lamplight, passing in and out of lightness and dark. The horses were walking, but they showed they'd also been sweated earlier. When the driver eased in at the plankwalk in front of the office a greaseboy ran out with a lard bucket and a flat stick. Two hostlers bustled out of the back lot with fresh teams, and a clerk wearing elegant lavender sleeve garters and carrying a clipboard, walked from the lighted office. The clerk looked up.

"Any passengers?" he sang out.

The driver yawned, stretched, and when he was good and ready, answered back. "Nope. You got any for the north run?"

"Three," stated the clerk, making a notation upon his clipboard. "An' you're seventeen minutes behind schedule." He turned and marched stiffly back into his

118

office leaving the driver and shotgun guard sitting up there bitterly eyeing his retreating back.

While the horses were being hitched Henry stepped up to Langston and said, "Thornton. It's ten miles west of Wellesey where this stage will leave us."

Langston looked at Henry. "You get that from Frank?"

Henry's nod was solemn. "He was very cooperative, once I explained to him I had to know where they were heading."

"Yeah," muttered Langston dryly. "I can imagine. What's at Thornton?"

"Fresh horses hid out at a deserted ranch, some food and other stuff. They're professionals all right."

Markley walked over and Henry went silent. But Tom Markley was not naive. He eyed the brothers and said, "All right; we're in this together, remember. What's going on?"

Langston repeated everything Henry had told him. Markley listened, and dropped a curious look at Henry just before the driver sang out, then all three of them walked over and climbed aboard.

They had the coach entirely to themselves. As they were whipping northward through the starry night Langston replaced his bloody and ragged shirt with the new one. Tom Markley hooked long legs across upon the far seat, slumped far down, tipped his hat forward and folded his arms. He was in need of rest. They all were. Before the stage had covered two miles they were sound asleep.

Men had to be both desperate for rest and hardened to discomfort to be able to sleep like that. All of them qualified on both counts. Even after midnight when the coach slowed to make the steady climb through the

119

northward pass and reached the heights where cold waited, none of them awakened. They were bucketing down the far side being flung from side to side as the roadway turned and twisted, before Henry, jolting sidewards, hit his brother's bandaged arm, awakening Langston. The night was wind-washed high up and crystal clear. Where the moon stood, peaks were south of them. From that Langston surmised they were nearing the town of Wellesey. He'd only been over there three or four times and remembered the place as being about like Minton.

When the driver called out a fluting curse at some lagging horse in his hitch, Tom Markley jumped wide-awake. Langston said, "Easy; it was just the whip cussin' at a horse."

Markley rubbed his eyes, spat through a glassless window and vigorously scratched his middle as he peered around. "Where are we?" he asked.

"Below the pass heading for the flat country south of Wellesey," answered Langston, who bent to nudge his brother awake. "No reason for you to sleep when Markley and I can't," he said as Henry opened one puffy eye.

Markley made a cigarette, lit it, made an awful face, killed the thing and threw it out the window. After that he sat straighter, and twisted to poke his head far out to see ahead. Instantly, he withdrew it.

"Wellesey dead ahead," he informed the others. "This coach must've traveled tonight."

"Last night," corrected Henry, prodigiously yawning. "Sheriff; you ever been to a place called Thornton, west of Wellesey about ten miles?"

Markley had been there. "You name a town within a hundred miles of Minton," he stated, "where I haven't had to traipse out some time since I took the lawman's job, and I'll eat your hat. As for Thornton, it's nothing. Just a well stop on the old time emigrant trail. They say at one time it had a dance hall and a dozen saloons. But last year when I was over there, wasn't more'n five or six families still living in the place, and all around are abandoned homesteads."

"That's just it," muttered Henry. "Frank's description of the abandoned claim where those horses are waiting was damned vague. All he was certain of was that there was a big salt lick on the place where folks had quarried the stuff years back leaving a sort of pit in the ground."

Markley yawned, again. "That'll be enough. But before we head for Thornton let's get something to eat in Wellesey."

The driver sang out again as they straightened up from the last curve and headed arrow-straight for the darkened town on ahead. The coach slowed, which was the custom, so the walking horses would be cooled out when they arrived at their destination. That was the longest mile of the entire trip, but it ended, eventually, where the stage ground up through a dusty, empty roadway and veered to the west plankwalk and halted where two smoky lamps hung on the front of a small office.

As stage line men came out on the left side, Langston, Henry, and Tom Markley got out of the coach on the right side. Markley paused to point up where a liverybarn stood in mid-square, then turned and pointed southward where a little hole-in-the-wall all-night restaurant stood. They went first to the restaurant where a sharp-faced individual bursting with curiosity, served them and got no answers to his probing questions. They ate in total silence with the caféman hovering nearby, paid and

121

walked out of the café feeling a lot better if they didn't look any better.

Up at the liverybarn they had to shake the cot inside a harness room to awaken the old codger blissfully snoring there, and after he was awake the old man venomously glared at them, obviously angry at being so roughly awakened.

"Three horses and saddles," Tom Markley said, holding his badge of office under the old liveryman's nose. "And if you have three saddle-guns we'll rent them too."

The old man got up, squinted around, made his quick judgment of the three strangers and said, "I got two carbines and a scattergun, Sheriff. How'll that be?"

"Fine," Markley said, holding the harness room door. "Now let's get rigged out and riding."

As the liveryman stumped out into his gloomy runway he said, "Sheriff; what's it this time: Rustlers, cowthieves, bronco redskins or maybe a murderer?"

Markley briefly considered the old man then dropped his head and in a low, conspiratorial tone said, "This is official business an' not to be passed along. It's all four—and abductors too."

The liveryman rolled his watery old eyes and went trotting down his runway. He suddenly halted six feet along, turned and said quizzically, "What's an abductor, Sheriff?"

Markley glared. His big voice boomed. "Get those horses saddled or I'll ab-ductor you!"

The liveryman jumped and ran on again.

They walked back out by the doorway while they waited. Wellesey lay dark and hushed around them except across the road and southward where the stage was having its horses changed and some mail sacks loaded on top. Even the saloons were dark. Markley looked at his watch, pursed his lips and said, "If we make good time and if *they* haven't pushed too fast, we'll make it all right, and that's figurin' a couple of hours or more to locate the abandoned homestead they're heading for."

Langston was unperturbed. "We'll make it," he murmured, somberly gazing across the road at nothing. "I'm wondering how those girls have made it."

Henry turned as the liveryman called to them. "Marci's tough," he said, and went with his companions down to where the liveryman stood. He had slung two saddle boots from a black horse and a sorrel one. From the big pig-eyed bay horse he'd tied the shotgun to the saddlehorn with a leather thong. He handed the reins around and Markley ended up with the ugly bay and the scattergun. The liveryman had extra cartridges which he doled out. He raised his thin face saying, "Sheriff; do I got to put in for one of them territorial warrants to get paid for all this?"

"Not a territorial warrant, a county warrant," growled Markley, turning his big bay and eyeing the beast askance. "But if this damned jug-headed varmint bucks me off you'll have to sing for your money." He stepped up and settled lightly over the saddle. The bay rolled its eyes and switched its tail, but did not move.

Langston also mounted. As he did so he said, "Don't fret. If there's any trouble or delay in you getting your money, send a letter to Langston Gunn over at Minton with the bill. I'll send the cash right back."

The liveryman perceptibly brightened. "Good

hunting," he said, and followed the horsemen out into the dark roadway where he stood craning after them to ascertain which direction they took. He'd have plenty to tell his cronies in the morning.

Markley hadn't exaggerated. He knew the country. Where the land ran westerly almost flat, he swung southward towards the dark-hulking yonder foothills where the going was rougher but safer. No one would be able to inadvertently spy them as long as they had those backgrounding rough slopes to blend against. It might have been an unnecessary precaution but neither of the Gunn brothers commented. Better to be absolutely certain they were safe than to risk having the outlaws know they had spent the night getting around them.

They passed a ranch were a dog caught their scent and raised Cain with his barking. They had to feel their way when the land broke up into criss-crossing erosion gullies below the forested foothills, and once they came upon a black bear who'd made the dangerous mistake of leaving the mountains and the trees.

"Calf-killer," growled Henry Gunn, riding with a hand instinctively upon his six-gun. But they did not fire; they perhaps could have, but they didn't.

The bear was astonished at their appearance. He reared up on his hind feet sniffing. At best, his eyesight was weak, but on a dark night his only thoroughly reliable sense was his nose. He was large, near six feet tall, and correspondingly broad. There were few things in this world he had to fear, but the smell of mounted men was one of them and he knew it. With a low grumble he dropped down, turned and went shagging it off back towards the uplands.

They had an interesting few moments while their horses recovered from the terror all horses feel for bears. Tom Markley kept a wary eye on the little nervous ears of his powerful bay.

Nothing happened. They eventually passed another ranch, also dark and still, but some corralled horses caught their scent and distantly whinnied. After that they were compelled to ride down into a broad, deep gully and up the far side. A mile farther on there was a creek to be forded. After that Markley jutted his chin through the gloom saying, "We're getting close. There's an old gaffer up here in Thornton who was a lawman down on the border years back. Whenever I've reason to ride over this way, I usually stop and palaver with him. He could know where this salt ranch is we're looking for."

When they finally saw Thornton it looked even more deserted and dilapidated than ever. In daylight it might not have seemed so bad, but in that pewter light with the great, formless shadow of the mountains lying over it, the place looked like a genuine ghost town.

Once, obviously, it had been a thriving, fairly large frontier post, but with the new road going straight over the pass from Wellesey, Thornton had died. It was a painful and lingering passing though, for while most of the homes, stores, outbuildings, were slowly decaying, there were several well-kept homes along the main thoroughfare, and a dog barked as soon as they came within hearing distance on their shod horses.

Markley halted. Langston was on his left, Henry on his right. They looked tough and capable in the gloomy night. Until Markley had completed his study of the onward town and lifted his rein hand to proceed, Langston was quiet, but after Markley was prepared to

125

go ahead, Langston reached over, brushed the lawman's sleeve, twisted and pointed. Off in the east the sky was steadily brightening.

"If this ranch we're hunting for is another ten miles off, Sheriff, there's a good chance the outlaws, up high in the hills, will spot riders heading for it."

Markley nodded but didn't speak. He set his course southward out over the plain towards the most dilapidated end of Thornton. Wherever that dog was he kept at his baying. When they finally got near their destination, though, he stopped, the stillness swooped down and covered everything. It was an eerie place to be in the small hours of the night, a forgotten ghost town far from the traveled roadways.

Markley made his final halt beneath a huge old tree, got down and hooked his reins over a low limb. They were behind a shack with a sagging roofline and a small fenced in garden plot where vegetables flourished but not a single weed showed in the soft starshine.

Markley led the way to a warped rear door and gently rapped.

CHAPTER SIXTEEN

THE MAN WHO ANSWERED TOM MARKLEY'S KNOCK at the door was tall, gaunt and slightly stooped. But he had a .45 in his right fist that never wavered, and neither did his steely eyes. It required a moment for him to recognize Markley, then he grunted, pushed the six-gun into his trouser waistband and stepped back.

"Come on in," he said, shuffling away in an ancient pair of felt slippers to grope with a coal oil lamp. "You sure come callin' at odd hours, Tom."

126

Markley introduced the Gunn brothers. The old man gravely shook hands and just as gravely looked them up and down. "Once," he said, "I knew a feller by the name o' Templeton Gunn down in Texas. But that was a long time back."

"Yeah," mused Langston. "A long time back, Mister Travis. Before the war on a spread northeast of Pecos."

The old man gazed at Langston from over by a little iron stove where he was poking up coals and pushing in more wood. "He kin to you boys?"

"Our father."

The old man finished at the stove, set the coffee pot on and motioned around to some rickety old chairs. He seemed to have turned reflective. While Markley made a smoke and the other two waited a trifle impatiently, the old man said, "Rode with Templeton Gunn in Mexico back durin' the other war. Later on, we crossed trails on the north plains huntin' Comanches." The steely eyes shifted. "Tell me he's dead now?"

Langston nodded.

"Yeah," the old man whispered. "Sure. All of 'em. I'm the only one ain't got the plain decency to die." He rallied with an effort as the coffee pot began to boil. "What's on your mind?" he asked Tom Markley.

"An old claim somewhere hereabouts, Travis, where four outlaws have horses hidden out." He explained to the old man why they wanted those outlaws. Finally, he explained about the salt quarry. Not until he mentioned that did old Travis's eyes brighten.

"Sure," he said. "The Holiday place. Folks name o' Holiday squatted there twenty years back. Then they pulled out when the town commenced to get poorly, like most everyone else."

"Where is it?" Henry Gunn inquired, bringing the old man's thoughts back.

"Four, five miles west at the foot of the hills." He gazed at Sheriff Markley. "You can't miss it, Tom. Go straight along the edge of the forest until you come to an adobe house and a log barn. It'll be the only adobe house you'll see in these parts. Them Holidays, they was from south Texas." Travis smiled. "They made their barn of logs all right, but they said adobe houses never burnt an' bein' that close to the forest a man had to sort of keep that possibility in mind."

Travis went over, silently filled four tin cups and silently passed them around. Afterwards, seated again in his chair and nursing the coffee while he studied his callers, he said nothing although it was very clear his curiosity was up.

He was one of the old ones who never asked personal questions.

Langston finally explained, when Tom Markley did not seem about to, that the men were coming over the mountains and should reach that Holiday homestead some time in the afternoon. Travis listened, thought, then nodded and sipped coffee.

"You'll get 'em," he ultimately opined, with full confidence. "They picked the Holiday claim because it was closest to the trees where they can just slide out 'thout folks spying them. But that works both ways: you boys'll be hid too, all the way along the foothills. The outlaws'll be above you, but you'll be cut off from their sight, providin' you don't dally. I'd suggest you get out of Thornton too, before daylight. I don't know there's anyone here who'd likely be in league with those men—but I don't say it's not possible either."

As old Travis finished his coffee he arose, gave his

shaggy head a hard shake as though regretting that he couldn't go along on this manhunt, and crossed over to pitch his tin cup into a bucket half-full of water.

Markley walked over too. As he put aside his cup he said, "We're obliged."

Old Travis gave him a wry smile. "Next time don't scare a man to death slippin' up on him in the night." He let the smile fade and looked over at the Gunn brothers. "You're in good company, Sheriff, if they got any of their pappy in 'em."

The three from Minton left Travis and rode out of Thornton with the first strong blush of new day on their left. That dog barked again, at the north end of town, as they passed upcountry heading for the shadowy forest where the foothills abruptly dropped down and flattened out.

Langston wondered as they left Thornton, and kept looking back, but if they'd been observed no one came out for a better look, and after they were well northward, he saw no horseman lope out of town westward.

Markley knew this upper country too, it seemed. He avoided all the pitfall erosion gulches passing in and out of the trees with the sun finally coming up to strike them across the shoulders.

By the time they reached the Holiday ranch the sun was well up. They'd moved up into the forest at Langston's suggestion to cover the final few miles, and they'd also halted back up in there to silently sit their horses and study the onward deserted ranch with its adobe house and massive log barn, before riding on down to where they came upon a southward trail leading back up into the mountains beyond the scrub oak foothills.

It was an old trail, somewhat overgrown, but it was nevertheless usable. Markley was thoughtful about that before he backtracked, cut northward out and around, and came into the ranch's deserted sun lighted yard well away from where anyone might inadvertently see their fresh tracks.

They found the horses—five of them—in a patched old pole corral out behind the barn where someone had plugged the holes in a trough and filled it. There were two manger-type cattle feeders in there chock full of timothy hay.

"Thought of everything," Henry mused. "Not just the hay and water either; those are damned good horses. I doubt if anything we're riding could even begin to catch them."

Back in the barn they paused in moldy shade to consider. Langston was of the idea they should take their mounts off a mile and hide them in the trees. "If they nicker when the outlaws ride in it'll be a dead give-away. And remember, it's not our lives alone we're gambling with."

"I don't like the idea of being left afoot," argued Tom Markley, but in the end he conceded. "Let Henry take 'em away," he said. "You and I'll do a little exploring."

Henry rode one and led two as he retraced his way back east beyond the ghostly ranch, then northward into the yonder forest. Langston and Tom Markley got up into the barn loft, found nothing but owls' nests, some rotting old harness straps and some musty hay. They crossed over and entered that adobe house.

"It's Texas," mused Langston. "The walls are three feet thick."

There were two bedrooms, a parlor, a kitchen, and a storeroom out back. The place was built like a fort. It

130

faced both the northward plain and the southward forested mountains.

"No one was goin' to slip up on Mister Holiday," mused Tom Markley, poking his head past a doorless opening. "Hey, look in here."

It was one of those small box-like bedrooms and in a dark corner a piece of soiled canvas lay atop some alforjas. Langston went over and pulled off the canvas. Markley gazed a moment then dropped to one knee, reached forth and opened the first pack bag. He held up some tins of fruit and beef, tossed them aside and held up an oblong, flat and heavy smaller box.

"They've thought of everything. Plenty of grub and plenty of ammunition." As he tossed down the bullet box and shoved upright he said, "Be damned if I can understand why they also raided my jailhouse office; they got enough ammunition here to wage a small war." He grunted. "Even bandaging. Lang; these are real renegades."

Langston tossed the canvas back the way it had been and walked out of the little gloomy room behind Markley. In the doorway he said, "I hope professionals get careless or sleepy or hungry just like novices, Sheriff. We're going to need a pretty solid break to catch them off guard enough to save those girls."

Markley said nothing. They returned to the yard and met Henry returning on foot lugging his carbine. He gestured up the slope. "Nothing coming as far as I could see and hear."

It was then close to high noon.

They made a careful survey of the place and ended up in the shade out back of the moldy-smelling log barn in soft quiet where they had the best southward view of the uplands. There, they made smokes and loafed in the

131

shade. Henry fell asleep. The other two let him slumber.

"It's hard not to try an' form some kind of a plan," murmured the lawman, squinting up against the sunsmash where it struck high up the yonder mountainside.

"We'll have time for that when we first see them coming down through the trees," surmised Langston Gunn. "In cases like this a man's foolish to try and hold to a plan anyway."

Markley looked over. "You sound like a man who knows," he said, eyeing Langston clinically. "You ever in law work?"

"The army," stated Langston. "But I reckon in some cases there's a similarity. Anyway; I've set up ambushes before. Not with girls' lives at stake though."

"Me too," Markley muttered. "I don't like it, either. If there were four of us to their four I figure we could pick them off. But three to four leaves enough leeway for error to get the girls killed by the survivor."

Langston said no more for a long while. He sat there feeling drowsy with his shoulders to the barn facing southward. The mountains were less densely wooded on this side than they were on the Minton side. Clearings appeared here and there, some well up the hazy slope, some clearings down near the foothills where few pines grew and more oaks darkened the lifts and breaks.

The sun hung directly overhead for a long time. Henry finally awoke, thirsty, and went around where that trough was out back. The other two left their shady place too, went along to the front of the barn and paused there when Henry called out from the rear of the barn.

"Look up the mountainside to the east a little. Watch those clearings up there. I could swear I saw horsemen about as big as dolls crossing a meadow up there."

As Langston turned he said, "How many, Henry?"

"Dunno, Lang, just riders. It was one of the smaller clearings. They went across it almost before I was plumb sure."

Langston considered. The clearings were several miles off, but what made it difficult to correctly gauge the distance was the fact that they were uphill. Still; he thought it would be another hour, and he said so to Tom Markley.

The sheriff agreed. They stood a moment watching. Henry walked through the barn and emerged between them. He pointed to a particular clearing. "That little one halfway down." He dropped his arm. "Follow on down slope with your eyes and you'll see a regular string of those little clearings all the way down to the meadow above the foothills."

Markley stepped inside the barn and gestured for the others to do the same. He gave no reason for this and neither of the brothers made any particular issue of it, either, although it had occurred to each of them that men as careful in their planning as those outlaws had already proven themselves, were not at all unlikely to possess binoculars.

Langston finally picked up moving little shapes skirting another clearing. He pointed them out. All three of the waiting men counted them this time: Six riders.

"That's our outfit all right," murmured Tom Markley. "They're just about on time, too. It'll be mid-afternoon by the time they get down here." He twisted and gazed upwards where the hay-loft door was, then he dropped his head and looked elsewhere. Langston, anticipating Markley's thoughts, said, "We'd better not get into any spot where we can't maneuver; that loft would be such a place. So would the adobe house. We've got to stay together and able to move if we have to."

Tom Markley said nothing. He kept eyeing the yonder slopes. Henry Gunn too, probed the uplands for more signs of those approaching riders. There was of course some consolation in the knowledge that they had outguessed the renegades, but professional murderers were not the kind who wouldn't be as alert as hawks and as deadly as sidewinders, so, although the Gunn brothers and Sheriff Markley had managed to get around them on their flight out of the Tanawha country, all that actually ensured was a showdown, with the lives of two girls at stake.

It was the waiting which got the three of them; the waiting, the full knowledge of their responsibility, and also the fact that they had no plan. Tom Markley made another cigarette and smoked it. Henry checked the carbine that old man back in Wellesey had put into his saddleboot. Langston strolled out back, got a drink of cold water and returned. The sun dropped off-center and began its hazy slide off towards the distant west.

Heat danced out in the yard, the horses out back occasionally squealed and stamped, and the last time the waiting men spied their enemies with the hostages, the six riders were close enough to the foothills to make a head-count very easy. That was when Langston said, "Take your choice; we can try an ambush in the foothills, or wait somewhere down here and hope they'll relax once they're afoot."

CHAPTER SEVENTEEN

"AFOOT," SAID TOM MARKLEY, killing his second smoke. "With luck we can keep them afoot, too, but first off we've got to get the girls away from them."

Langston turned and said, "Follow me."

He led them on westward beyond the barn, beyond the corral out back to a shallow erosion gulch he'd noticed earlier when he'd walked behind the barn to get a drink of water.

They got down into the arroyo and turned. They commanded an excellent view of the ranch, the yard, the outback corral and even, by walking northward, the runway leading through the barn from back to front.

Markley leaned over, placed his scattergun across the top where the land was flat and squinted around. Behind him the land was open for possibly twenty yards, then a little hill stood up with chaparral up its side, and some juniper trees atop it. The land seemed to grow progressively wilder the farther west they looked.

Southward of course were the oak-studded foothills and above them, the forested mountains. Northward the land was more open. It had trees and land swells and brushy growth too—even some trees—but it was by far the most open country except for that easterly countryside they had ridden parallel to from the town of Thornton to reach this forlorn spot.

Langston said, watching the slopes north and east of them from the arroyo, "I doubt that they'll waste a lot of time here. They know we're after them."

Henry corrected that. "They know *someone's* after them."

Markley finished his long study and picked up his shotgun again. "They won't head eastward or they'll be seen at Thornton."

"Westward looks pretty rugged," Henry mused, gazing off in that direction. "It'd be good hidin' country, but what these men need is country they get over fast. The west's too rough for that."

Langston tipped his hat brim down to shield his eyes as he kept watching the foothills where those riders would eventually come down into the open out of the forest. "That doesn't leave much," he exclaimed. "Northward. They just came over the southerly trails from Tanawha Valley." He paused when something moving caught and held his attention. Then he went on speaking as before. "They'll stop here to eat, change horses, maybe rest a little if they're confident they've got the time. Then northward again up through the breaks." Langston broke off again, staring up where afternoon shadows lay like tan shade among the mottled low rises among the foothills. Then, as before, resumed speaking, but this time his tone had noticeably altered; become more incise, more hard and sharp. "If they abandon the girls here—fine."

Henry grunted. "You don't think they will do you?" he asked.

"Of course not," growled Tom Markley. Then he said, "Langston; what do you see?"

The answer came in short sentences, as an artillery spotter might have spoken to aim a cannon. "Beyond the adobe house a half mile. To the right where three oaks stand atop an east-west low ridge. Watch

136

around the upper slope. They'll be riding out in a moment." Langston turned. "You two satisfied we're in as good a spot as possible?"

Markley didn't answer at once. Neither did Henry. They instead concentrated upon that place where the horsemen would appear, and they did; they came riding around the sunshine side of the hill one at a time looking tired and disgruntled and used up.

As he watched the horsemen, counting and straining to discern the two girls, Markley said absently, "This is as good a place as any, Langston. If we have to, we can drop back to the little hill behind us. If they get nosin' around we can fade out in the chaparral."

Henry had his own notion of why they shouldn't seek a different place. "We can see the horses in that old corral. If we're ever going to catch 'em off guard that'll be the time—when they're saddlin' up."

The riders came steadily ahead. Their animals were finished; they walked head-hung and scarcely lifted their hooves but rather dragged them forward scuffing dust.

The men rode two in front, two farther back. Between them were Marci Colburn and Evelyn Hunter. It struck the crouching watchers that the girls seemed to have weathered that terrible ride up and over and down the mountainsides far better than the outlaws. Either that, or the girls were making a brave show, and their captors didn't give a damn how they looked, because the closer they came to the adobe house the more obvious it became they had no inkling anyone might be watching them.

They passed around between the house and the watchers, were lost to sight for a while, then emerged heading for the barn. They stopped, finally, looked around and heavily dismounted. Not a one of them said anything, They moved like men who knew exactly which move to make, and when to make it, without talk or even thought. One of them, a lean, willowy blond youth, jerked his thumb at the girls. They also got down. Finally, as they were off-saddling, the whiskery one Langston recognized as the man who'd waylaid him across the mountains, said something.

"So far so good. I'm hungry enough to eat the soul out of a saint."

That seemed to break the mood. An older man, big and heavy and with a very small, lipless mouth among his otherwise generous and coarse features, and, "Let's give the ladies a chance to show whether or not they can cook."

The fourth one was a stooped, venomous man who wore his dark hat pulled so low he had to tilt his head to see the others. He too was unshaven, but he looked as though being dirty was something he'd choose, rather than as something he couldn't avoid. "I got a better idea for them females," he snarled. "An eye for an eye."

The willowy fair youth turned, his face expressing disgust and weariness both. "What the hell's wrong with you," he rapped out at the venomous-looking one. "We already talked that out. Frank took his chances just like you did an' I did."

"Don't mean we can't even things up a mite for him, does it?" demanded the venomous man, glaring from the off-side of his bareback horse. "Anyway; you figure to keep these damned females with us? You know cussed well they slowed us every foot o' the way. I say—"

"Ease off," rumbled the large man with the petulant, selfish little mouth. "We'll eat first. Then

138

we'll talk. An' personally, as far as I'm concerned, all I say is that we stick to that schedule we worked out before we hit Minton. It worked slick as a charm over there. It'll work just as well at them other towns. By this time next year all four o' us'll be drinkin' champagne out'n silk slippers on the Barbary Coast o' San Francisco, with more damned hard money in our pokes than we can spend in a couple years. Now let's get some grub. Come on; leave the damned horses. We don't need 'em anyway. When we pull out we'll use the fresh ones."

The big man turned, stepped away, looked back and slowly, blackly scowled. The others obediently started along too. It was the fair youth with his notched, tied down .45, that said something to Evelyn and Marci, then herded them along ahead of him.

When the girls passed back across the yard between the head-hung, listless horses at the barn, and that old adobe house, Langston, Henry and Tom Markley got a good look at them where the sun brightly shone. They were grey with fatigue. If they'd looked less than worn out before, it was now very clear this was only because they'd been perpetuating that kind of an act.

Markley's lips formed some unspoken words, then he shifted his attention to that willowy, blond youth strolling behind them. "There goes three thousand dollars on the hoof," he murmured. "That lanky blond feller is the Texas Kid—wanted from here to Idaho for everything in the book. You name it."

"Recognize any of the others?" Henry asked.

Markley shook his head where he crouched, leaning upon his scattergun. Langston said, "The short one with the reddish stubble walking ahead with his friends— that's the one that waylaid me over the mountain and

139

gave me Evelyn Hunter's scarf."

Langston turned, no longer watching the outlaws and their hostages. He tiptoed down the arroyo until he could see up through the barn where those exhausted horses stood. When the others slipped on down there, having lost sight of the renegades as they'd entered the adobe house, Tom Markley said, "They aren't expecting a damned thing. We can set them afoot with damned little effort, Langston. Open the corral gate and hoorah those horses they showed up here on."

This was what Langston had also been thinking. But he had an objection, too. "They'd guess at once someone had caught up and gotten around them. As long as we can't keep them from harming the hostages we're going to have to let them get even more careless."

"And if they don't?" Markley demanded.

Langston looked at him. "They've got to. But if they don't, then we Indian-stalk them after moonrise tonight."

Henry nodded. "Catch 'em in their soogans," he agreed. "As tuckered as those four are they'll be sleepin' like babies."

Markley stepped away in thought. Clearly, Langston and Henry had a point; after their harrowing ride, the outlaws would rest well. Even if they posted a guard, which they'd probably do, he wouldn't be any fresher than the others. Markley beckoned. The three of them returned to their upper vantage point in the arroyo. He twisted to cast a look off where the afternoon sun was beginning a long, swift slide down the reddening late-day sky.

But although men may deserve success they cannot command it; whatever Tom Markley had in mind for

140

the three of them when they returned to the lower end of the wide, grassy arroyo, was not to come about, for two of the outlaws strode forth from the house with Winchesters. They stopped and without speaking looked all around. One of them stepped down into the dust and quartered back and forth, up and down. It was late in the day for reading sign but this one tried. Then the second one walked on out, raised a hand to shield his eyes and peered up towards the easterly foothills. The first one came up. They talked for a moment, and in their arroyo Langston, Henry and Tom Markley watched those two with dawning comprehension: something inside the house had tipped the renegades off that others had been in there.

"Let's hope," muttered Henry, closely watching the two armed men up in the yard, "they figure it was just some nosy rangeriders who came and went on."

Langston had no comment about that. Neither did Markley. Of the pair of them, Langston's carbine was the only weapon that would reach those two in the yard. Markley's scattergun would make mincemeat of men at fifty, or perhaps seventy-five feet, but after that the pattern of its shot diffused too much."

"Headin' for the barn," murmured Henry, as those two out in the yard turned and hiked off side by side, still looking left and right. "They're sure spooked!"

"You would be too," muttered Markley, "if you had hangin' over your head what those two have."

Langston watched the renegades enter the barn. He moved suddenly, without alerting the other two, ran down their arroyo until he could peer up through the barn and watch the renegades. He acted as though he was fearful those two might get out of sight. Markley and Henry Gunn hastened after him. When the three of

141

them came together Langston pointed. One of those outlaws was watching the adobe house, the other one had put aside his carbine and was in the corral with two ropes stalking a pair of horses.

"Be damned," breathed Henry. "They're pullin' out on the other pair. Something in the house gave them a bad upset."

"Our tracks in the dust," muttered Tom Markley. "Or maybe because we didn't put the tins back in the alforjas that we took out."

Langston was thoughtful until the two outlaws led their animals into the barn to saddle up. As he watched, peering through the descending gloom, he said, "They've split up the money; either on the trail somewhere or just now in the house. Otherwise these two wouldn't pull out." He gestured for his brother and the sheriff to drop down. "They're comin' this way from the back of the barn."

"Dammit," growled Tom Markley, raising his shotgun. "They'll force a fight sure as the devil when they see us in here. The shooting'll warn the others an' it just might get those girls killed."

Langston motioned for Henry to move farther northward. He flagged Tom Markley farther southward. Ahead through the dusky shadows those two riders were more carefully looking back than forward, which is unquestionably what prevented a gunfight, for when Langston Gunn rose up with a cocked Winchester to confront those two, their horses shied back and halted in astonishment before the riders even looked forward to see what had occurred. When they did look, it was no longer safe to draw guns, or for that matter, even move a gun-hand. To their left a bulky, unsmiling man seemed to sprout forth from the very earth. He had a

142

double-barrel shotgun trained upon them from sixty-five feet away. To their right a thick-set sturdy cowboy had them covered with another Winchester.

The eldest of that pair was the same man who'd given Langston Evelyn Hunter's scarf across the mountains. He puckered up his eyes as he also slowly raised his hands up to his shoulders. "Hell," he breathed softly. He had recognized Langston; he just didn't quite believe his own eyes that Langston was standing there in front of him.

The other one was that venomous man, his narrowed eyes as hooded as the eyes of a hawk. He was slower lifting his hands but he lifted them. "I was right," he whispered. "There *was* someone here, and they didn't pull out."

Langston gestured. "Get down." He tipped back his head. "Henry; Sheriff; come closer. Don't shoot 'em if they make a bad move—club them to death." Henry and Tom Markley dutifully came up closer. The outlaws stepped down. The mean-eyed one kept muttering oaths under his breath; he was fearful, but more than that, he was disgusted.

CHAPTER EIGHTEEN

TOM MARKLEY GRABBED THE REINS to the outlaw horses, moved around and tossed them to Henry. Tom then ungently yanked away the six-guns from each outlaw and shifted his shotgun to his left hand, drew his own six-gun and without a word struck both the renegades from behind. The first one to fall was the venomous-eyed one. The other one, beginning to twist away, took his blow down the side of his head.

Markley didn't even look at the Gunn brothers. He simply knelt, hauled at the belts of the unconscious men and began systematically and efficiently to bind their ankles and arms. Langston went over to assist, saying nothing. Whether he approved or disapproved of the way Sheriff Markley had acted he gave no sign of it. Henry led the horses down into the arroyo and southward where there was brush to tie them to. As he hastened back his brother and Markley had rolled the renegades down into the gully. They were trussed like turkeys and each man had his own bandanna knotted around his lower face.

Still without speaking, they took the guns from their unconscious captives and checked their loads. While they were doing that Langston said, "We can't wait any longer." Markley agreed with a grunt and turned to lead on up out of the arroyo towards the corral, and beyond the corral, to the log barn.

They got to the corral without incident, but as they were stealthily moving towards the barn a man walked forth over at the house, looked, saw them moving, and sang out.

"Hey you two; chow's ready. Find anything?"

Langston called back. "No," and stepped inside the barn behind the other two.

"Told you," called out the man up at the house. "Just some nosy rangeriders. They come, looked around, and rode on. Come on; let's eat an' get to ridin'."

They passed silently up to the barn's front entrance, peered out, and watched that man over at the house saunter back inside. Henry let out a long breath and leaned upon his carbine.

Langston moved ahead, got around Tom Markley

and halted when he was out of the barn. There was a pale yellow glow of flickering light coming from the house. "Candles," he said.

Markley too stepped out, but as he did so over at the house two silhouettes suddenly appeared around the far side of the house. Markley, seeing how those two glided along, each with a Winchester in his hands, whispered, "Look out," and eased back inside the barn.

Langston also stepped back inside. He and the others exchanged a look. "Your voice didn't sound right," speculated Henry. Langston shook his head in doubt about that; how could someone saying just one short word from behind a log barn sound much different from anyone else?

"I don't think that's it," he whispered. "From the house that first one could see there were only two horses left in the outback corral. He didn't let on. He went back inside and told the other one their two friends were trying to pull out."

Markley said, "The girls; if those fellers think they're only fightin' among themselves, the girls will be safe in that adobe house." Tom moved forward and crouched to peek out into the yard. From across the yard a gun flashed and roared. Markley staggered backwards throwing out both arms. Henry lunged, caught the lawman around the middle and spun off to one side with him like big Tom Markley was no heavier than a sack of grain. From out in the darkness a man yelled over: "Run out, will you?" And called Markley a string of sizzling names. "Steal the best horses and try to leave us, will you?" That invisible man drove another bullet down through the barn.

Markley angrily pushed away the solicitous hands of Langston and Henry Gunn as he straightened up. "I'm

145

not hit," he hissed. "It just startled hell out'n me. I wasn't expecting anything." He dusted wood dust and splinters off his shirt. "But it was damned close," he muttered. "Watch that one, boys, he's one hell of a good shot."

From behind the barn a gun exploded. The second outlaw was guarding the pair of remaining horses in the corral. Langston motioned for his brother to watch the rear doorway as he sidled up towards the front entrance. There were no windows in the south side of the barn, otherwise Markley might conceivably have crawled out and flanked one or the other of the outlaws.

The talkative one out front kept calling names and making threats. Langston was certain from the strong, youthful sound of that voice, the one out front was Tom Markley's Texas Kid. He'd seen just enough of that one to have a very wholesome respect for the Kid's gun prowess.

The one out back began swearing too. Langston paid this one no great attention. When he was close enough to get belly-down and remove his hat, he risked looking carefully out into the darkness. There was no way to determine where the Texas killer was unless he fired. Even his shouts and taunts did not pinpoint his position. Langston thought he was constantly moving over yonder where the darkness was thickest, so he lay perfectly still, waiting for a red flash to fire at.

It didn't work out that way. From behind the barn someone let off a big squawk and tugged off a swift shot, levered and fired again. First a shotgun roared, sounding as loud as a cannon inside the old barn, then a six-gun added its dull, throaty crash. Both Henry and Tom Markley were back there. Evidently the outlaw back by the corral hadn't expected two men to so

146

savagely attack him. He fought back but he also kept howling for the Texan to hurry around and give him some support.

Langston eased out his carbine. He was certain, since the Texan also thought it was the other two outlaws inside the barn, not three strangers, that he'd rush forward. But the Texas Kid didn't; the reason he didn't was at once made clear when he sang out, his voice vibrant with quick alarm and strong suspicion.

"Hey; who had that shotgun? Didn't none of us have any scattergun. Hey; who's inside that damned barn?"

Langston's hopes flickered out. The Texas Kid was too chary, too alert and observant. Langston dropped his head low, snugged back the Winchester, and waited. One way or another, the Texas Kid would have to do something. He did; he got off two fast shots that sang right on through the barn from front to back. Langston squeezed off his own shot while the winking blaze of that second shot was still visible. He levered and threw more lead into that same identical spot. Someone over there fell or stumbled or flung down a gun; it was a hard, abrasive sound. Langston sprang to his feet. He expected the Kid to make a break for the house where the hostages were. They were his only ticket to safety now, and he obviously knew it.

Out back those three men were savagely swapping lead. Evidently Henry and Tom Markley had the other outlaw pinned down so he dared not try to get clear.

Langston saw a blur of movement heading southward. He dropped to one knee, aimed and fired. The shadowy blur jumped, lit down, whirled back and snapped off two six-gun shots. One ripped into the wood six inches from Langston, the other one passed on by. Langston didn't flinch; he had to stop that man short of the adobe house. He squeezed off another shot. That one drove the outlaw flat down, out there, where he viciously fired twice more, and rolled. Langston could hear his spurs rattle against the hard earth. It wasn't much to go by but he flung aside the Winchester, yanked one of the guns taken from the first two outlaws from his waistband, drilled three shots, one left, one right, one plumb center, over where the sounds had come from. That time there was no reply.

He gingerly arose, stepped along the side of the black front log wall, where he blended into the formless gloom, and flattened when a shot came searching. He answered that one too, and hastened away. Again the Texas Kid fired and again Langston answered him. He had one slug left in the gun he was holding. It occurred to him as the Kid fired one last time, what the Texan was up to baiting Langston into firing his gun empty. He obliged, fired, tossed the six-gun down and drew his own forty-five.

It wasn't a very long wait. The Texan uncoiled up off the ground and sprinted hard for the house. Langston tracked him where he passed beyond the shadows out into the starshine, and fired. The outlaw lunged far over, staggered to his left, turned as though in utter disbelief that anyone could reload that fast, and fell. He was no more than ten feet from the open door of the adobe house.

Out back the surviving outlaw was still bawling for support where Tom and Henry had him mercilessly pinned down. Langston considered going back to help with that one, but in the end he decided to make certain the Texan was dead. If he wasn't, he was much

148

too close to the house to take any chances with.

Langston reached the end of the barn. When he went away from there he too would be in that same pewter light. He hung still and watchful for a moment trying to detect movement across where the Kid lay. There was none. He took one short step, then another. Nothing happened. He started in a darting, erratic run. Still nothing happened. He made the complete crossing and dropped his cocked six-gun the moment he could see the Texan's face. There was no need. That lethal shot had clipped the Texas Kid high in the chest from back to front. He was dead. Out of habit Langston bent, scooped up the outlaw's six-gun and flung it away. Then he turned and called out.

"Henry! Tom! That one you've got out back is the only one left. The Texas Kid is dead!"

Almost at once the outlaw behind the barn bawled out that he'd had enough, that he'd surrender if Henry and Sheriff Markley would let him. They called to him to stand up without his guns. The last shots left only their diminishing echoes as Langston strode on past, entered the house, and called softly to the girls.

"Evelyn? Marci? This is Langston Gunn. Where are you?"

They came timidly from a rear room, ashen and shaken, one of them holding aloft a little candle. There was a smell of cooking inside the house. There was also a smell of burnt gunpowder. The two girls stood solemnly looking at him as though incapable of believing their eyes. He went across to them and as he did so loud, growling voices outside sounded from the yard. The girls cringed.

Langston said, "It's my brother and Sheriff Markley

from Minton. Nothing to worry about."

Evelyn lowered the candle. Her large eyes were nearly black. She was totally expressionless. Marci, shorter, quicker to recover, alternated between watching Langston and the yonder doorway where those voices were coming up. He finally also turned. As he did so Henry and Tom Markley shoved a disheveled, hatless, unshaven big hulk of man through the doorway. They had taken the precaution to wrap the renegade leader's arms behind his back with his own gunbelt. The girls flinched from the outlaw's wild glare.

Markley reached out, rapped the big man sharply with his pistol barrel and said, "Sit down. Don't open your lousy mouth. Just sit down there on the floor and be quiet." To Langston, Tom said, "How're the ladies?"

"Look all right," was the quiet reply. "Shaken, but able to navigate."

Markley nodded. "Good. Henry; let's go fetch the pair we left sleepin' in the arroyo."

As his brother and the lawman departed Langston gazed at the big outlaw where he was slumping down. The man only looked up once, then averted his head and slouched against the wall.

Evelyn Hunter placed the candle upon an old box, walked over and leaned forward to kiss Langston squarely on the lips. He was startled and showed it. Marci came over too, but she had to stand on her toes and brace with both hands flat against his chest. He flushed scarlet but it was too dark to notice that. He made a little self-conscious chuckle.

"Reckon I'd go through it all over again," he said gallantly, and asked them if they'd been hurt in any

150

way.

They hadn't Marci assured him, then, as though a dam of silence had been breached, they threw questions at him without allowing time for the answers. He explained how they'd come over the pass in the night; how they'd pushed hard to reach the old abandoned ranch before full daylight, and finally, he told them how they'd known where the outlaws were heading. That was when the prisoner lifted his head to also listen.

Evelyn Hunter said, "Langston; I'm thoroughly ashamed for what I thought—what I almost had the others do to you."

He felt for his makings and went to work fashioning a cigarette. "You know," he told the tall girl, "ever since I first noticed you, Miss Evelyn, I've had a sort of feeling some day we'd sort of cross trails." He popped the smoke into his mouth, lit it, exhaled and eyed the tall girl with a little, sardonic smile down around his lips. "But the way it finally happened—well, ma'am—I don't expect I'd be up to having to go through that again, for quite a spell."

Marci smiled, then slowly lost her smile as those two tall people gazed straight at one another. She finally turned and stepped across towards the door where Henry and Sheriff Markley were approaching from the direction of the arroyo with two unsteady, bound captives in front of them. She moved out into the yard and smiled as Henry came up.

"Uh," she said, "maybe you'd ought to stay out here for a few minutes, Sheriff: Mister Gunn. Uh— the other Mister Gunn and Evelyn are—well— they're sort of renewing acquaintances."

Tom Markley stopped and scowled. Henry didn't scowl

but he too stopped. Little sturdy Marci, the way she was standing there with tawny moonglow touching her close-cropped red-auburn hair and her grey-green eyes, was a sight to distract any man.

Markley's scowl went away. He looked from Henry to the girl and back to Henry again. He mumbled, "I'll go round up the horses. I'd like to get back to Wellesey and head for home after we turn the critters over to the liveryman over there. It's still goin' to be a long . . .a long . . .' Markley reached out, shoved their two wobbly prisoners to the ground, growled: "Stay there!" And turned abruptly to go back over towards the barn where some of the horses they'd need still were. All the way across the yard he waggled his head from side to side. Men like the Gunns went through hell's fire and brimstone, getting shot and shot at, and when they saw two girls they'd seen a hundred times before, all of a sudden it hit them.

"Be damned," Markley growled to himself as he stepped inside the barn. "Be *double* damned!"

We hope that you enjoyed reading this
Sagebrush Large Print Western.
If you would like to read more Sagebrush titles,
ask your librarian or contact the Publishers:

United States and Canada

Thomas T. Beeler, *Publisher*
Post Office Box 659
Hampton Falls, New Hampshire 03844-0659
(800) 818-7574

United Kingdom, Eire, and
the Republic of South Africa

Isis Publishing Ltd
7 Centremead
Osney Mead
Oxford OX2 0ES England
(01865) 250333

Australia and New Zealand

Bolinda Publishing Pty. Ltd.
17 Mohr Street
Tullamarine, 3043, Victoria, Australia
(016103) 9338 0666